THE DAMNED ONES

Also by Mary K Gowdy

The One and the Other Series

The One-Sided Coin (Volume One)

Poetry

Sensuality.

*Where Have We Come From,
Where Are We Going?*

THE DAMNED ONES

A ONE AND THE OTHER
NOVEL

MARY K GOWDY

ISBN 978-1-7349505-0-2

Printed and bound in USA

10 9 8 7 6 5 4 3 2 1

Cover Design by Agata Broncel, Studio Bukovero
Proofreading by Emily Gowdy and Dale Smith

*To the women in my family
who have kept fighting
when the world has tried to crush them.*

Tet-qua
The Northern
Castle
Regemir
Laluv Forest
The Toun Cliffs
Jous
Resenmir
Ilion
Cuv Gulf
Vresn Mts
Phesellen
Ithli
Annameen
Soros Cereminir
Nixceenac Mts
Ilsaphanor
Rilias Islands
Loreiak

With wings that brush like needles of pine,
in smoke it flies for eyes can't confine
its faithful form. Its voice can tear thy soul,
*   one strip heaven-bound,*
*   one strip made Unfound,*
to taste again the light for sin it sold.

For ev'ry man and woman'n child fair,
the watchmen light the briars'n call, "Beware!
Go and close your windows sound and hope in thee
*   they do not creep,*
*   in thee they do not sleep.*
The slaves of Darkness roam, the Jemalgee!"

For when they enter, they will devour
thy goodness, and thy sweets will turn sour.
When through our mirrors they peer into all,
*   like a tower crumbling,*
*   like a river rumbling*
o'er cliffs, the shards of thy mind will fall.

\- a folk song,
origins unknown

Dior

The girl steps onto her chamber's balcony with nothing over her nightgown to shield her from the autumn night chill. The laces of her hiking boots are undone. Though I can't see what happened inside her rooms, I can guess that her muscles have withered too much for her to tie them. The dark rings around her eyes have grown since I saw her last, and her blonde hair has turned black. She's grown gaunt from carrying the burden of you, nothing left but bones and the skin to cover them now.

You coil around her in a cloud of smoke, cloaking her form in your darkness so no eyes, human nor mine, can see her. Your darkness catches on the shadows, pulling them toward you like a cloak snagged on a tree branch. To the palace guards and servants, there is no part where the night ends and you begin. But I see your shape and know the reek of your souls. They've become one like you had hoped—in a way. In the way a boil is one grotesque appendage pulsing its poison into its host. I'll let you guess which one is yours.

No one but I senses Loreiak's forsaken princess—their Unfound princess—jump off her balcony. They don't know how her body dissolves into the same black smoke and drifts to the ground unharmed. She is no longer the human girl with those blue eyes that you swore saw the good in all, but for those few moments, she is you, a Jemalgee with blood on her hands as old as the earth. Long ago, you entrusted yourself to the Ghustaugness—the darkness that makes even the flowers shrink and die. And the Ghustaugness now lives in her, reshaping her more in its image every hour.

Her feet reform, and the pine needles crunch as she becomes weighted again. You lead her through the garden's terraces that climb the slope of Mt. Raseynor, moving your black smoke so it hides her at all times. It isn't until you've reached the edge of the gardens and the beginning of the trail that you lift the veil. There are no walls on this side of the palace grounds, though there is still some obsidian dust left over from when they used to cast their mystical borders to keep us out. The priests have let them fall into disarray and uselessness now that the creature they fear most lives inside their princess.

She is panting and has to use her hands to climb though the elevation is not that steep and she used to navigate it with ease. You take her to the place where you first met. The stream always seems to appear out of nowhere. The water tumbles down in short steps, curving sharply and racing past. It rushes over the cliff to her left and thunders down against the water a hundred feet below. Her brow dampens with sweat and spray.

Sitting so close to the edge of the cliff that it appears to defy gravity is a smooth boulder—her favorite writing spot. It's big enough for at least three people to comfortably sit and pinches in the middle like a bean, providing the perfect seat. Its pale sandy color would glow tonight if there were moonlight and starlight to reflect.

Do you bring her here because you wish to ask the stars for mercy again? They no longer hear you.

Only I do.

And I spit on your prayers. I vowed that I would hide the stars' faces from you if you chose her over me. After everything I followed you through, the exile I shared and suffered by your side, you abandoned me for a naive girl's promise of redemption. You were a fool. I told you again and again that there was no fighting against our natures. Once the Ghustaugness enters, it devours.

And is that such a bad thing? We had good times, didn't we? We had pleasure, power, and dreams. We could've had more.

(Maybe we still can.)

I. hate. you.

I hate you.

Denying myself all the pleasure of the world to make true my vow has not been enough to satiate my wrath. It does not inflict the level of pain you cause me every time you deny me. I've plotted ways to torture you more, but there's no point. For nothing could please me more than getting to watch this moment as you destroy the girl you so severely loved.

TWO AND A HALF YEARS EARLIER

I

As Princess Reshelia Redyian dressed for her wedding later that afternoon, one thing was on her mind:

Where in the found world was her sister Labeth?

No one had heard from nor seen the crown princess all day, and the three courtiers whom Reshelia had sent to find her came back empty-handed. Labeth would conduct an important part of the ceremony—a part that the queen normally would've done, but their mother had decided that Labeth should perform it this time in preparation for her future responsibilities. Labeth hadn't taken the hint.

When the fourth courtier came back with no news, Reshelia couldn't take it anymore. She jumped to her feet as her hand-maiden moved to put the crown of Leedathou flowers on her head, causing the woman to stumble backwards, and proclaimed that she was going to find her herself. "I am not letting her ruin this day."

"We searched her rooms and the rest of the palace grounds. She's not anywhere," said a courtier as she passed.

"She's my sister. I'll know where to find her better than anyone else."

The handmaiden chased after her. "Wait! Your Highness! Your cape!" The magnificent piece of silver velvet dragged on the ground for several feet behind her, but its makers had never intended for it to *touch* the ground. It needed two servants—no more, no less—to carry it. It was quite heavy, loaded as it was with jewels of sapphire, diamond, and amethyst along with detailed embroidery. But the cape's weight didn't slow Reshelia down, for the threat of a slightly less than perfect wedding day will give any bride stamina no matter how tight her bodice is. The handmaiden managed to grab onto its end, but she was huffing by the time they reached the crown princess's chambers.

Labeth was neither in her sitting room nor her bedchamber, so Reshelia checked the balcony. The noon sun blurred her vision, so she had to shield her eyes and squint to make out anything. The woods behind the palace were a dark green, having soaked up all the spring rain, and their thin branches swayed in the breeze. Clouds glided in under the blue sky, blown in from the sea a day's travel to the south.

In the middle of the balcony was a trash basket, its bottom littered with crumpled pieces of paper. As Reshelia leaned in for a closer look, something bounced off the back of her head followed by a squeak. She turned. Sitting on the roof was Labeth—

journal and quill in hand, ink pot perched inside the gutter by her bare, ink-stained feet. "I'm so sorry. I didn't mean to hit you. I was aiming for the. . .um," she motioned widely, her cheeks reddening. "I can't remember the word. Which makes sense considering I can't think of the right words for anything now."

Fists on her hips, Reshelia gave her sister her best disapproving glower. She shouldn't have to explain why she was angry.

"It's time for me to get ready, isn't it?" Labeth asked.

"The time was several hours ago."

"And I'm so sorry." Labeth grabbed the ink pot, and as she jumped down from the roof, the jolt splashed ink onto the balcony, inches away from Reshelia's silver dress.

The bride flinched away like a cat from water. "Labeth! Be careful!"

"I'm so sorry," Labeth repeated, but when she stepped forward, Reshelia retreated.

"Don't get any of that on my dress!"

The handmaiden still holding up the cape shuddered. "Don't even speak of it, Your Highness. That would be a disaster."

"I just want my wedding to be perfect," said Reshelia tensely.

Labeth shrank back. She knew how much this day meant to Reshelia. She'd been talking about her wedding since they were children, so much so that Labeth would've paid her to shut up about it. And when she'd met her groom, Hithlin, the longing looks they gave each other were the stuff of epic romances. For Hithlin's happiness, Reshelia would do anything and vice versa, but there was never reason for toil nor sacrifice because just having each other made them so happy.

It was a very special day, and Labeth needed to not get any more in the way.

"I'll go get ready," she said, rushing to her bedchamber.

"Your dress is in my chambers," Reshelia reminded her.

"Right." She turned on her heel to head for the door.

"The stars know I wouldn't want you preparing yourself for this," Reshelia said as she picked a pine needle from Labeth's hair. Even without turning to see her sister's face, Labeth could hear a faint smile in her voice and the tension diffuse. While they fought like normal sisters, hard feelings didn't stay for long between them.

"You're going to wear flowers in yours," Labeth jabbed back.

"It's a ceremonial headpiece. Yours is a few needles away from becoming a bird's nest."

When they reached Reshelia's dressing rooms, their mother, Queen Anallia, was waiting for them. She'd been adjusting the dress of their teenage half-sister Asanilph when they entered. Asanilph rolled her eyes, annoyed with their mother, but the queen never noticed. Labeth's late entrance in her obvious unprepared state—pine needles, bare feet, and all—was much more deserving of her immediate disapproval. She didn't say a word, though. She didn't have to.

"Mother," said Labeth, her voice breathy with embarrassment, "it's good that you're here. I was just about to get ready."

"The wedding starts in a couple of hours."

"So there's no time to waste." Labeth hurried into the bathroom. Anything to get away from that stare. She stepped into the lukewarm bath that had been drawn for her, and the handmaidens began shampooing her scalp and scrubbing her skin.

"Where were you?" her mother's voice came from the other side of the door.

"In my rooms." The resounding silence communicated that her response was inadequate. "I was trying to write something. But the words just weren't coming and I lost track of time."

Her mother sighed, a familiar sound. "You need to be more responsible."

"I understand that. I just—."

"Well, clearly you do not if your sister has to hunt you down when you are needed."

While her body was getting cold from the lukewarm water, her face burned. She wanted to be a good queen, but the day-to-day responsibilities bored her. She'd rather be writing. And most of her "responsibilities" were adhering to court niceties rather than working on anything meaningful. She tried to care and to do what was expected of her, but sometimes it was hard to drag herself away from the page.

Before she could reply, the handmaiden pressed her head underwater to rinse the shampoo out. When she resurfaced, she heard her mother say, "We'll talk about this later."

"Yes, Mother," she replied, thankful it was over for now.

The handmaidens pulled her from the bath and lathered her in lotion that sparkled with gold flecks before fitting her in her dress. It was a grape-like purple, the color of royals, with tiny square jewels of gold sewn onto the bodice. The neckline bared her shoulders but rose all the way to her neck where there was a gold collar covered in diamonds. Two pieces of sheer fabric ran from its back and attached to each of her wrists, also collared in diamonds. At both of her temples, gold pins in the shape of butterfly wings pinned her wispy blonde hair in place though it hung freely down her back. The handmaidens painted her eyelids a dark purple and her lips a wine red. When Labeth saw herself in the mirror, it relieved her to see that the handmaidens needing to hurry hadn't detracted from their skill at all. She looked just as good as she would've if she had arrived on time. Everything would be fine.

Her sisters and mother had also finished getting ready. Asanilph wore a flowy, lilac dress that accentuated her youth with its modest neckline and puffy sleeves, something Labeth was sure irritated her. At fourteen, Asanilph wanted to be treated like a woman and had a habit of acting out to prove just how mature she was.

The queen's dress was the darkest purple and wrapped around her elegant, thin frame. Fine gold thread like a collection of tiny rivers accentuated its folds where it gathered at the waist. Pins positioned her hair atop her head, but she wore no crown. The only jewelry identifying her as queen was a long diamond chain necklace with a four-pointed star jewel that hung near her navel. She looked so regal, but it wasn't the dress nor the jewelry that made it so. It was in how she carried herself, from the angle she held her chin to how she moved her hands when speaking.

But Reshelia was the most magnificent looking of all of them. Both her dress and cape were silver, the color customary for brides. The heart-shaped bodice and sleeves left her shoulders and neck bare where a large necklace of interlocking oblong shapes fastened the cape. In the middle of the dress's neckline sat a pendant of several tiny sapphires, all different shapes and sizes but fitted together in a circle. The pleated bodice blended into the flowy skirt that stopped around her ankles. Set atop the sleeves and skirt was a thin layer of silky lace with designs of flowers and vines. Perfect corkscrew curls framed her face which had been painted to make her eyes shine, her cheeks rosy, and her lips a gentle pink. Her skin had also been lathered with silver flecks like Labeth's had been with gold. On her head was a crown of purple Leedathou flowers that would open once the sunlight touched them. All of her dress accentuated the beauty of the delight in her smile and in her eyes.

"You look gorgeous," Labeth told her.

"I ought to be," Reshelia replied, glancing at the grandfather clock. "It's time to leave. The carriage has been waiting. Let's go." She turned toward the door with a flourish of her hand.

As Asanilph came up beside Labeth, she whispered, "You'd think she were the queen by how she acts."

Labeth gave her a side eye. "It's her special day. Just let her have it."

Asanilph rolled her eyes, and they followed their mother and sister down to where a carriage awaited them. The base was made of white wood carved with scenes depicting all four seasons as they were experienced in the mountains around their city of Soros Cereminir, the capital of Loreiak. A dome of white cloth shielded them from the wind and made the carriage look like a giant egg shell. Inside, they sat on plush couches set into the carriage's frame. It was spacious enough for them and the two handmaidens still holding Reshelia's cape. Eight horses pulled the heavy carriage.

On the ride through the city, Reshelia waxed poetic about how overjoyed she was to finally see the day where she and her beloved would pronounce their undying love for each other and celebrate their union with the whole city. The wedding would take place on the main thruway of the Temple District on the slope of Mt. Vashilien. Five main mountains surrounded the city and Lake Urvuspha. The palace occupied the second highest point of the city, halfway up Mt. Raseynor. Then, Mts. Rel and Odons to the south framed the main road into the valley, and across Lake Urvuspha rose the cliffs of Mt. Jakor, which had been a volcano before most of it had collapsed several millenia ago. The lake had formed over its remains.

Though only nobles would witness the ceremony, the whole city prepared to celebrate. All businesses had closed early, and the people crowded the streets to watch the carriage pass. Cheering, they threw flower seed in the air that pattered down the carriage's roof like soft rain. Labeth laughed, and Reshelia stuck a hand out to wave at the people.

Once the carriage pulled inside the Temple District, attendants rushed Labeth's sisters away to a nearby temple, and Labeth and her mother ascended the main thruway where the ceremony would be conducted. The path was wider than most of Soros Cereminir's roads and was split into eleven large platforms by short staircases. Each platform possessed a carving of a Dual, a pair of things, one being mystical and the other seemingly mundane. Though they seemed different, the people of Loreiak believed that they were one and the same. Blood was life just as words were power and smoke spirit.

Many pathways diverged from the main, leading to various temples, monuments, and statues. While there wasn't much in the way of gardens, some of the tallest pines in the city grew in the Temple District. Dozens of acolytes were busy sweeping away their pine needles. The highest point of the city was the monument of The Celestial. It stood at the top of a steep staircase carved from the mountain itself. Its eleven white stone pillars created a perfect circle and towered over everything. They even blocked the sun, and in the shade of one stood High Priest Dlanacen.

He was an older man, balding on the top of his head and graying on the sides. His stiff red robe with black tassels and embroidery indicated his standing in the priesthood. The regular priests wore black. Bowing, he greeted them with their titles. "I've arranged the wedding table." He motioned to a table beside him with the various objects he and Labeth would use while co-officiating.

"It looks perfect. Thank you," said her mother.

"Will Her Highness still be the one conducting the ceremony?" Dlanacen asked.

"Yes," her mother replied.

Labeth wished she had answered herself. She hated it when her mother and other officials would talk about her like she wasn't there. It didn't matter that she was now twenty-one. The habit had never faded out of existence.

"You remembered to rehearse the procedures on your own, Labeth?" her mother asked.

When she had messed up the rehearsal with Dlanacen a few days prior, they had settled on Labeth practicing more later. "Of course," she replied, just then realizing that she hadn't followed through. "But it wouldn't hurt to go over it one more time."

There was only one hour left till the ceremony's beginning, and Dlanacen filled that time with refreshing Labeth's memory. But it was the prime time of the day for grogginess, so it was hard to concentrate. Even in the shade of the Celestial, the day's warmth and humidity sank into her skin. As her underarms grew damp, Labeth found a new appreciation for her dress not having sleeves.

She was so focused on getting everything right that she didn't notice the guests trickling in until she looked up to see that the seats were packed. Her heart fluttered. She didn't know why she was nervous. She'd been in front of crowds before as the crown princess, and this ceremony was small—only a few hundred people, most of whom she knew. Her friends Josa and Osilor waved at her from their seats. She gave them a wink.

The ringing of a gong followed by a brush of wind chimes marked the beginning of the ceremony. Everyone went silent and turned in their seats to watch the procession. A woman dressed and painted in gold danced down the aisle, scattering flower petals across the walkway. After her came two priests swinging thuribles burning incense, and then one person of kin for both the bride and groom followed, Asanilph for Reshelia and the groom's father. Finally the bride and groom themselves proceeded up the walkway between the pews. They walked one foot apart without touching, their hands clasped in front of them. The groom, Hithlin, was a handsome, kind fellow with a square face that was pleasant looking but not striking. And Reshelia with her beauty and standing could've easily had someone striking, but she'd chosen the one who made her the happiest. She couldn't even keep her eyes off him though her attention was supposed to be on the officiators. Labeth didn't mind. She loved her sister so much it was impossible to not be infected with those same butterflies.

Dlanacen explained the importance of marriage and how each object in the ceremony symbolized them becoming one. As he talked, Labeth's thoughts drifted. As crown princess and queen, she wasn't required to marry, but she did need to produce an heir, preferably a daughter. Of course, Labeth wanted to fall in love, but she could never shake the feeling that marriage wasn't in the cards for her.

She shivered as the last dregs of winter bit back in a cold wind before fading to spring's warmth. All over the mountains, the trees chattered a chorus of leaves. Labeth stared at them, transfixed. She didn't understand why. It felt like, for a second at least, something had brushed alongside the innermost part of her. Her soul.

"Your Highness?"

Whatever it had been was gone. It was so brief, she might have imagined it. She'd never—.

"Labeth!" came a growled whisper.

Reshelia was glaring at her, her jaw clenched. Beside Labeth, Dlanacen had picked up a knife and was also staring at her. On the table in front of her was an identical knife. She snatched it up; it was the beginning of her portion of the ceremony. How long had she been distracted? Hopefully not long enough for people to have noticed. But Labeth knew, despite her best wishes, that it had been.

The knives were crude, made of dark gray stone and attached to wooden hilts wrapped in leather. The blades were flat and coarse but not dull. They were made to look ancient but were not so. Tradition required that they look like the knives made by the people of old to represent how marriage was an age old tradition, but the frequency of weddings required that new ones be made as old ones became too bloodstained to be used for centuries. It was unsanitary as well.

Labeth cut her sister's palm while Dlanacen cut Hithlin's. "It is tantamount that the bride and groom not touch each other during the ceremony before their blood has been joined," she explained. Labeth took a small jar made of cloudy glass and squeezed her sister's palm so several drops of blood dripped into it. Dlanacen repeated the process with the groom's hand. "They are two separate entities, and the mixing of their blood will usher in the mixing of their lives. And their souls."

Afterwards, the couple bandaged each other, reciting the vows of protection, loyalty, and companionship that would come in a marriage. While they did that, Labeth and the High Priest corked the jar, sealed it with candlewax, and placed it into a bag of dirt that they gave to the new couple to keep somewhere safe in their home. The couple were to plant a flower in the dirt, for plants were the dual of time. The seed thrown as they had ridden through the streets represented the new beginning of the marriage, and the flower petals cast along the aisle symbolized how nurturing their love through commitment to each other would produce beauty. The flower they'd grow in the dirt would forever be the representation of their marriage. As their marriage lasted, strengthened, and changed, so would the flower.

Reshelia took the bag while Hithlin grabbed her other hand. When they turned to the crowd with their clasped hands raised, everyone cheered. The festivities could begin.

Her duty done, Labeth could finally relax. It was Reshelia's day so everyone was fawning over her, and the crown princess was beneath their notice for once. Which was great considering she and her friends had some plans which required them to sneak off once the wedding feast was over.

"This lamb is delicious," said Josa as she took another bite of the tender meat. "And I can't believe how many desserts they have." In addition to the delectable meats, fruits, and soups on the table were multiple small cakes, pies, and pastries.

"They certainly spared no expense on this wedding." Osilor, Josa's lover, swirled the red wine in his gold-plated goblet before taking a sip and dabbing at his thin, black mustache.

Throughout the Temple District's gardens, guests lounged on piles of pillows and cushions at low circle tables made of grayish-white marble, each encircling a tall black lantern holding a candelabra, its staff etched with flowers and vines. The candles gave everything a soft orange glow as the sun set behind the mountains, painting the sky layers of pink, purple, and indigo. The bride and groom sat at the table at the highest point of the hill, while Labeth and her friends' table was placed to the side where not many people would pay attention to them.

"Of course they didn't! It's a momentous occasion. A wedding." Josa sighed, her gaze far off and dreamy. "Everything's been so marvelous. The flowers, the dresses, the decorations. And not to mention how sweet it is when two people pledge their love to each other."

Labeth gagged. "You sound like my sister."

"I'm only mentioning so, you know," Josa fiddled with her napkin, "in case it gives anyone ideas."

Osilor chucked, taking Josa's hand and massaging her knuckle with his thumb. "Alright, hint taken. But I think it's best to wait till we know more about what's going on with the Toa. I could get deployed."

Even the mention of Loreiak's neighboring country quickened Labeth's heart. They had never been at war during her lifetime, but the Toa were threatening it. They'd sunk one of Loreiak's largest merchant ships, unprovoked. Around the same time, the Toa had stopped trading with Loreiak, which caused some anxiety as their nation was becoming increasingly dependent on the technological advances they'd acquired from them. A few cannons had since been fired, but Labeth's mother and her advisors wished to settle this matter with diplomacy rather than bloodshed as soon as possible.

"We should go ahead and do it then," said Josa.

"I don't want to rush things," Osilor replied. "You should have as marvelous a wedding as this one."

"Just don't ask me to officiate, please," said Labeth.

"But you did such a great job," Josa told her.

"Did I really?"

Josa's reassuring smile faltered.

"How bad was it?"

"You did zone out for maybe, like, five seconds. But other than that, you were wonderful," her friend rushed to add. "Though you could tell that Reshelia was a bit mad."

The night's darkness came fast, and now that the sun was fully gone, a cannon shot golden sparkles of fire that exploded in the air. The first dance was beginning. Along with poetry, dance was one of the most treasured art forms in Loreiak. Everyone learned how to take part in the intricate group dances. Even though Labeth and her friends were familiar with the steps from their childhood, the dancing figures still commanded their gazes. As they silently watched, Labeth resorted to fiddling with the flakes of her jelly-filled biscuit rather than eating it, her appetite killed by guilt.

"Do you ladies want to dance?" Osilor asked.

Josa pursed her lips. "It's too formal here for me. Why don't we go somewhere else?"

"I was waiting for you to say that," he replied.

Turning to Labeth, Josa smiled closed-lipped and mischievously. "You ready?" The rest of the city would've joined in the revelries by now as their taverns, bakeries, dance squares, theaters, and more opened their mouths wide to be filled with merriment and celebration. Labeth and her friends had planned for weeks to cast off their status and slip into the city to take part.

"Let me speak with my sister first," she replied. "And then, I'll meet you in the Acolyte Quarter."

"Perfect! Don't be too long."

Josa and Osilor hurried off to get changed—and maybe do some other things—while Labeth approached the bride and groom. Reshelia and Hithlin remained at their table with a rotating wheel of guests coming to congratulate them. Labeth eased onto the cushion next to Reshelia just as the lord of the Northern Castle excused himself.

"How does it finally feel?" she asked her sister.

Reshelia took Hithlin's hand while gazing into his eyes. "It's amazing."

While her sister's and friends' love-sick demeanors were cloying, Labeth felt like she was on the outside looking in, a little kid curious to know what she was missing. Even if marriage didn't seem right to her, that didn't mean love wasn't. Marriage was all about declaring the deepness of one's love for another, and Labeth also wished to be loved so completely.

"I'm so happy for you too," she told them. "You have my best wishes."

"I would hope so!" said Reshelia.

"Thank you," Hithlin added with a small smile as he gave his bride a teasing glance.

Labeth leaned closer to her sister and lowered her voice. "But I also wanted to apologize for messing up part of the ceremony. I know you wanted everything to be perfect."

Reshelia's happiness faded. "Then I don't understand why you weren't paying attention."

Labeth drew back, surprised at the biting words. She'd been expecting forgiveness. Reshelia was often quick to annoyance but she was just as quick to forgive. Usually.

"It's my wedding. But your mind was still on something else. It always is." There was sadness in her voice along with frustration.

"I'm so sorry—" Labeth began again as Hithlin caressed Reshelia's shoulder.

"It was a small mistake," he told her sister. "It didn't affect anything. I doubt anyone even remembers it."

Hithlin's words echoed Josa's reassurances from earlier, and it struck Labeth how believing that something was forgettable or beneath notice was an easy way to comfort. But it often wasn't true.

"You're right." Sighing, Reshelia took Labeth's hand and gave it a squeeze. "It's okay," she said, but for once, Labeth didn't believe her.

"I have to go." She pulled away.

"Don't get caught." Labeth had clued her sister in on the plan since its inception. Reshelia was also no stranger to sneaking off into the city. "Mother would have your head if you caused any scandal tonight." Labeth had a feeling that their mother wouldn't be the only one.

"I won't," she promised, a little hurt, and went to meet Josa in the Acolyte Quarter. A portion of the building had been reserved for the wedding party to finish getting ready during the ceremony, so now there were empty rooms where they could remove their jewels and change into simpler dresses and cloaks. They joined Osilor by the entrance with the least amount of guards and headed into the city.

Candles burned from every entrance and window so if looked at from the crest of a hill, the ground seemed to have as many stars as the sky. Balconies had their railings wrapped in garland, and celebrators shouted from them at the people below. Song came from everywhere—from the musicians on the corners, from private homes, and from taverns.

In every major square, there was dancing. The people of Loreiak loved group dancing, and the more people the better. It was normal to change partners ten times in one dance, and often the dances bled into each other so there was no need to stop. If one wanted to stop, they'd have to disengage during the few times they'd reach the edge of the crowd. They'd come, spit out by the stream of dancers and barreling out for a few steps before they could slow their feet. Many of the moves here had slight variations from the ones done in court. Where the nobles' dancing was more exact, technical, and formal, these dances were livelier, more playful, and had room for self-expression.

Labeth loved it. She had never felt like she'd had a complete picture of her country till she started exploring it disguised as a commoner. The passions, the smells, the tastes, the people found here were all things she could never experience as a crown princess. And this was the Loreiak she loved the most. If a queen needed to truly know her country, then sneaking off into it should be a requirement.

Once they were all sweaty and jelly-legged from dancing, Labeth and her friends headed into a tavern to grab some more wine and listen to people improvise songs or poems. After the third love poem, Josa leaned over to Labeth and said, "See anyone you like?"

"What?" Labeth sputtered.

"Love is the air. It might be your lucky night." She winked. Gesturing around the room with her glass, she said, "Look around."

Blushing, Labeth followed her command. There were many pretty girls in the tavern, but she wasn't sure about approaching any of them. She didn't have much experience doing such a thing nor discerning whether a woman would be interested. She was about to tell Josa to forget it when she noticed two women sitting in the darkest corner. The one with curlier hair rested her arm on the other's knees, her whole body attuned to the other. But the other scanned the crowd, her face expressing the epitome of boredom. Both had long blonde hair, tanned skin, and heart-shaped faces. They looked enough alike to be sisters. Labeth glanced down at her wine before the bored one's eyes met hers.

"Anyone look interesting?" asked Josa.

"Well—" began Labeth, and that's when she saw her sister. Asanilph. "What is she doing here?"

"Oh," said Josa when she saw the fourteen-year old taking a long gulp of something that wasn't grape juice. She was with two other girls her age from court. They'd changed into simpler clothes but had neglected to take off all of their jewels which would no doubt draw unwanted attention.

As Labeth went to confront her, Asanilph rolled her eyes and turned toward the bartender. "Can I get some more?"

As the bartender acquiesced, Labeth ordered him to stop, pointing out that Asanilph and her friends were too young. "The young lady asked for it," was all he said.

Labeth was about to command him again to stop but remembered that she wasn't the crown princess here. "What are you doing here?" she asked Asanilph.

"Having fun!" She could smell the wine on her youngest sister's breath. "That's what you're doing."

"It isn't safe for you here. You're too young. And I can tell you've already had too much to drink." Labeth reached for her glass, and Asanilph pulled it away and stood. Even being seven-years her junior, Asanilph was a couple of inches taller than her and had a pride and temper that was much larger. She was only Labeth's and Reshelia's half-sister. Their mother had conceived her with one of her past lovers. Her hair was more brown than blonde, and she possessed a sturdier frame than either of her half-sisters.

"Stop acting like Mother," Asanilph said. "And what does it matter how much I drink? I can do what I want here. There's no one watching me. Except for you," she sneered.

"You could be found out. You don't want to embarrass yourself."

"You're one to talk," Asanilph shot back. They stood so close now that Labeth could see the soft torchlight illuminating the drunken film over her eyes. "You can't even get your own sister's wedding ceremony right."

Labeth pulled back as the other girls snickered. For a moment, she did wish she was like her mother who knew how to command respect and put people in their place. No one had ever disrespected her this way since she was the crown princess. She didn't know how to respond. She felt like an embarrassment. She couldn't live up to the status of the crown, and everyone knew.

"Let's go," Asanilph said to her friends. As she lifted her bag from the bar, a block of chalk fell out. It dusted the front of Labeth's shoes. Before she could reach for it, Asanilph shoved it back into her bag. "Have fun. Hope Mother doesn't find out," she said overly cheerful. Almost kind of threatening.

Labeth shook her head and returned to her friends. Asanilph wouldn't tell Mother because it would expose her as well which meant Labeth couldn't say anything either.

When she returned to her friends, another performer took to the stage. "What would you be willing to bet that it's another love poem?" said Osilor.

The performer was an older woman with gray at her temples. Her black hair was thick and tied back into a ponytail, and beaded bracelets jangled on her wrists as her hands shook.

> "We swear to war," she began, "repaying their sick surprise,
> the goods they sunk, the blood they happened to have spilled.
> But no one hears the mothers' cries."

The room progressively fell silent with each line of her poem. To bring up the sinking of the merchant ship by the Toa and the impending war on the night of a royal wedding celebration was unexpected and jarring.

> "I have no ash to spread for my son lies
> in cold seas, somewhere."

The poet added the last word with palpable bitterness. Her voice trembled as she continued.

> "He screamed as he was killed
> but no one heard his cries.
>
> For greed, revenge, and pride more sons will die
> and us, their mothers, cry out as more ships are built,
> but no one hears."

When the woman rushed off stage, the room started talking again, first at gossipy whispers before rising to its previous volume as everything reverted to normal. Some jeering sounded from back by the bar though Labeth couldn't tell whether it was cheerful or affronted.

Josa touching her arm drew her out of her thoughts. "I'm sorry," her friend said.

"What?" Labeth replied, confused.

"I'm sorry you had to hear that. And on your sister's wedding day, too," Josa went on. "I'd be offended if someone criticized the crown for declaring war."

"We have to defend our country," Osilor added. "And avenge her son. What else does she want us to do?"

Her friends looked to her for a response, and she had one but not for them. She headed for the table in the back where the woman sat facing the wall, alone with a mug of ale. Labeth stopped abruptly a foot away, but the woman didn't look at her.

"I'm so sorry about your son," she said. To be offended by the poem hadn't occurred to her at all, for the woman's words had struck her with the horror of losing a child. She knew the woman must be experiencing unbelievable pain. She had heard it in the tone and weakness of her voice and in the diction and structure of the poem. When the woman remained silent, Labeth felt compelled to say more. "I want you to know that I do hear your cries. And I understand."

"Do you?" asked the woman, finally looking at her.

"Yes! I agree that war is not the answer. It only leads to more loss of life. And it's all only ever about greed and power, like you said." Labeth's words sped up as they carried forth her passion. It was a sentiment she had felt many times before but hadn't had the opportunity to express. "We need to stop it all."

"Do you know the name of the ship that the Toa sank?"

She searched her memory to find it, for surely something so important must be there. But it wasn't. "No," she admitted.

"Then you do not understand."

Humbled, Labeth sat beside her. "What was the name?"

"The Sunbound." Setting down her ale, the woman picked up a small jar with a tiny dose of a scarlet liquid. She twiddled it between her fingers. "There's not been an hour where I haven't remembered his face. Or how he liked to capture fireflies and light the living room with them. I worked my damnedest to make sure that nothing bad ever happened to him. That he could have a good life. But I could never really do that," she added, the bitterness back. "The world laughs at you if you try to control it." She dropped her hand holding the jar to the table with a thud.

Labeth wished to reassure her that she had done her best but kept silent for fear of sounding naive. "What is that for?" she asked instead, nodding to the jar.

"The last stanza of the poem:

> With this, I meet my memories' demise
> by wind, my tears, and blood to make my heart still."

And no one hears, Labeth thought, the ever-diminishing line finally gone. As her memories of her son would be with the ritual the woman planned to use, probably later that night. Rituals were the way to harness the power of mysticism, the magic of Loreiak, and usually involved a poem written by the caster and elements representing the Duals. Words were the Dual of power, so reciting a poem was the way to cast a ritual. To mix her blood and tears, her life-force and her grief, in the jar would create a concoction that when evaporated and swept away by the wind would take her memories with it. Wind was the Dual of nothing for it carried everything away.

"Why do you wish to take away your grief?" asked Labeth, surprised.

"Have you ever lost someone?"

"No." Now that the woman pointed it out, she felt embarrassed for asking. The pain of her grief must make it a compelling choice. "I thought you would want to keep your memories of him. It's all you have left."

"In a couple of years, no one will remember the name of the ship that was sunk or the sailor who was on it. The world may grieve now but it always moves on. Why should I be left with the pain?" The woman stared at Labeth with an intensity and a candor that made her uncomfortable. Her face was lined and her eyes bloodshot.

Labeth wanted to contradict her because choosing to forget your own son seemed wrong. But she had no words to explain.

A scream pierced through the bar followed by more cries. Several people rushed outside to investigate, and as Labeth craned her neck to see more, the woman slipped away. Thinking it was best to leave her alone, Labeth exited the bar with the others to see what was going on.

"Oh Stars!" screamed a woman. "Sholene! It made me—." The rest of the words were obscured by sobs that sounded like retching. Once outside, Labeth paused and shivered. She was curious to see what was happening but feared that she shouldn't.

In an alley were the two women Labeth had seen earlier, the ones who had looked enough alike to be sisters. One of them was the screaming woman, and she trembled, pulling at her hair and clothes, as she knelt over the dead body of the other. The dead woman's face now looked behind her.

Gasping, Labeth stumbled back, and thankfully Josa and Osilor had caught up and were able to keep her on her feet. Her heart beat so quickly, and a sick and weak feeling crashed upon her. Beside her, Josa sucked in a breath.

A man tried to comfort the crying woman, but she thrashed against him, screaming and sobbing at the top of her lungs. "My sister! It made me kill my sister!"

"What?" someone from the crowd shouted.

"It was a Jemalgee!"

Labeth thought she couldn't feel any more horror, but the woman's proclamation chilled her even more. Several people in the crowd bolted away, and the man that had gone to comfort the woman shrank back.

Osilor wrapped his arms around both Labeth's and Josa's shoulders and steered them away from the scene so forcefully they had to jog to keep up with his pace.

"Is anyone going to help the woman?" Labeth managed to get out.

"Forget about it. We have to get you out of here," Osilor said. "Jemalgee can read souls. It'll know you're a princess!"

And it would try to possess her. He didn't have to say it. Every child of Loreiak was raised to fear the Jemalgee. They were the oldest creatures in existence, immortal, unfathomable in size and yet able to be invisible in darkness because they were slaves to the ghustaugness—the ultimate darkness. They possessed whomever they liked to experience the pleasures of the world and make their hosts do whatever dangerous and demeaning things they wished.

A crown princess would make a prized host.

Labeth quickened her pace.

Dior

Do you know why I suggested we possess those two sisters that night? I had watched them and searched their souls for a week before to make sure that they were right. That their souls were pure. Innocent, young virgins just like you liked. With blonde hair. Like her. Though you won't admit it to me, I know the reason you take any host at all anymore is to drink in the light they possess. Since you can no longer be with our brethren in the sky or be one with their fullness of light, you've resorted to the morsels found in humans.

Your darkness is always too much for them. You drive them to commit horrible things and leave them with the madness. You made that girl snap her sister's neck because you were angry at me. I was trying to draw you out of your depression by remind- ing you of all the good we can still enjoy.

Let's eat, drink, and fuck for we will never die, I told you. For we've seen so many human ages pass and that's all there is. And love. My love for you will never die.

(Until you killed it).

That's why I kissed you in the alley. I wanted to make you happy, to moan with pleasure. You hadn't been interested in me for quite some time, and I had hoped the taboo of the incest would reawaken that hunger in you. You've expressed your dis- taste for it but that's not what you feel in the moment.

You said I didn't get it. How pointless our immortal lives are where we "ruin countless men and women to taste what we've eaten thousands upon thousands of times." And I had heard that a thousand upon thousand of times. Forgive me if I snapped at you for once. I merely yelled at you, but you, the one wanting to stop ruining people's lives, killed an innocent woman out of your pettiness.

You hate that you keep doing this, but you can't stop your greed. For a touch of Light satisfies you more than mine ever can. Though it is not as faithful as me. I think it's vanity to try to regain what we lost forever, but I gave you that woman anyway because I loved you. I was always patient with you as you crept back into caves to wallow in your guilt until another innocent soul seduced you back out.

(And I was always there).

II

WHEN THE JEMALGEE SIGHTING REACHED the queen's ears, thankfully there was nothing about Labeth and Asanilph being where it had happened. The queen sat on her silver throne, her back straight and jaw so tense Labeth swore she could see a vein pulsing. Upon finding out the next morning, she ordered the magical boundaries around the palace and Temple District to be strengthened. Various groups of guards and priests searched the mountains for it but had come up empty-handed. High Priest Dlanacen himself was now before Labeth and her mother in the throne room, providing their findings—or lack there of.

"It was too close," said her mother. "What if it had possessed one of my daughters? They've been known to pick on brides."

Seated to the queen's left on a smaller wooden throne, Labeth chewed on her fingernails. She'd been so close to them.

"We've talked to the remaining woman," continued Dlanacen. "It's hard to understand her as she's been hysterical since the possession. But she's finally admitted that there were in fact," here he paused, looking a little nauseated, "two Jemalgee. One in each sister. They hadn't attended the ceremony, just the festivities in the city." He added the last part quickly.

"Two?" repeated the queen, the word full of restrained anger.

"I'm afraid yes, Your Majesty."

"Find them and banish them to the Unfound World now!"

"Of course." The priest bowed his head and hurried out.

Once he was gone, the queen rubbed her eyes and temples. While she wasn't the most affectionate mother, Labeth knew how much she cared for her daughters by how hard she fought for their safety and their futures. Labeth didn't want to see her mother like this, but where the Jemalgee were concerned, fear was the appropriate response.

After a few moments, the queen straightened and returned to her regal composure as easily as if she was putting on a hat. She was dressed in blue silks with yellow embroidery. A lengthy train ran from her shoulders, twisted around her right wrist, and then fell to the floor, just touching the stone like a waterfall. She motioned the guards to let the next person in. They didn't move.

"Your Majesty," said the one by her right shoulder. "A delegate from the Toa has come to speak with you."

"What are they here for?" Labeth couldn't help herself from interjecting.

The queen only raised her eyebrows and took a deep breath, her skin paler. "We'll find out."

The guards opened the black doors at the other end of the throne room. The room was oval shaped and made entirely of dark gray stone. Pillars lined the walls at regular intervals and in-between their alcoves were lanterns held aloft by sculptures of tree branches. None of the lanterns were lit as they wouldn't do much to light the large hall. The ceiling let in all the light.

The pillars extended to the high ceiling where they seamlessly connected to arches that criss-crossed overhead. In-between the stone arches, the ceiling was completely glass. The glass was all divided into pieces like any stained glass window except the ceiling was made up of mostly clear pieces to let in the most sunlight. Purple, blue, green, and red pieces formed swirly lines that didn't create any big picture. Loreiakians loved their intricate, and sometimes random, designs. Instead of making their art into pictures, they preferred to let everyone find their own picture within the lines. It was another thing Labeth loved about her people.

The delegate would've stood out anywhere in Loreiak with his strange Toan attire. He wore a crisp and rather plain coat of metal gray over pants of the same color and a white shirt. Extending down the middle of his chest was a narrow piece of black cloth. His ruddy brown hair had been combed over a thinning scalp. On his face were these things Labeth had heard were called glasses. Monocles were a common thing in Loreiak, but ever since their country and the Toa had begun trading more, the rich had taken to these square frames that contained lenses for not just one eye but both and didn't require a hand to hold them aloft as the ears supported them. They were always a strange sight to see.

When he stopped before them, he bowed low to show respect. "It is a pleasure to meet with you, Queen Anallia Redyian. And Crown Princess Labeth."

"I'll have to admit," started the queen, "we had been planning on sending our own delegates to your country. We were not expecting your arrival."

"I'm sorry for the late notice, but the president felt it best that we not wait."

"What is your business, then?" Her tone was not hostile but lacked any of the fake politeness commonly used by nobles.

"We've enjoyed our special trading relationship the past couple of decades. Very few sections have been able to overcome their barriers to cultivate such a relationship with another." Before most of written history, a great, unkown force split their world, Azain, into several sections. Magical boundaries separated these sections so each was governed by its own rules of magic. Most could be divided into two types: those inhabited by a species other than humans with their own supernatural abilities or those with a type of magic that could be learned by anyone like Loreiak with mysticism. The section the Toa belonged to was an outlier. They had no magic but instead were blessed with technological inventions so far beyond the capabilities of the other sections that they may as well be magic. "When we first opened this pact, we figured it would be mutually beneficial. And your country has flourished with the introduction of our technologies."

"They've definitely altered our way of life in many ways," said the queen. Labeth noticed her careful rephrasing of the delegate's presumptuous claim. Loreiak had flourished long before they'd begun using the Toa's technology. And its introduction had caused many problems as well.

"We hoped in exchange," continued the delegate, "to take some of your magic back with us. A fair trade. But the barriers between your section and ours won't allow it. Every time we try to bring something over—a talisman, a ritual—they no longer work. We've tried everything. Your magic can only exist on your small continent. So we ask, kindly, that you give us the lands upon your eastern coast for a new Toan settlement."

"Excuse me," said the queen.

"It is either that or you fight for them."

"How dare you—?" began Labeth, but her mother covered her hand with hers. Labeth relaxed her fingers which had clawed into the wood.

"You may return to your country," the queen said slowly.

"And your answer is?" the delegate asked, unperturbed though he had just threatened war.

"I don't care what horrid machines you have created. This land chose us, and the blood of your soldiers will only strengthen our power."

Labeth wanted to gloat but settled for a smirk.

"Alright then." As he walked out, the delegate pulled from his pocket a small device which he broke open and fiddled with before pressing it to his ear and talking to it. Labeth had never even heard of such a device. So much for the Toa's generosity with their technology. There was so much the neighboring country had kept from them. Loreiak had discovered their submarines the hard way. What other weapons of war were they hiding?

Once the throne room doors closed behind him, the queen stood and ordered the scribe who had recorded everything to start writing letters to all of Loreiak's generals. Labeth came up beside her, her confidence deflated now that reality was setting in.

War. They were going to war. The blood given to the earth would not just be from the Toa's but from their own as well. From men—boys—like the woman's son.

"What are we going to do?" Labeth said.

Her mother squeezed her shoulder. "We're going to fight as if the Sandman himself were dragging us to the Unfound World."

Labeth tried to mirror her mother's resolve but the anxiety never went away. Only grew.

Labeth scratched out her last—and so far only—line of the poem she was writing. She hadn't completed anything in weeks, and what little snippets she managed to squeeze out were atrocious and infantile. Some thought or emotion in her needed to be poured out, but no words could capture its fullness, so she was stuck with its persistent yearning in her chest.

She threw her journal and quill down onto the rock she was sitting on. She'd gone to her favorite writing spot in her desperation, hoping that the setting would cure her writer's block. Far up the slope of Mt. Raseynor, outside the palace limits, was a thin but tall waterfall that spilled into a large pool which fed into the Yaynoxce River. A mountain path led from the edge of the palace gardens to the peak of the waterfall where a large boulder perched on the cliff's edge. Labeth liked to sit on it as she wrote.

She liked the soft rustling of the birds and raccoons, how the rock beneath her bare feet would grow cold as the night stretched on, and the stars. They and the moon were so bright that she only needed the lantern she brought for hiking through the forest and not for writing by. Up here, one could see how numerous the stars were as they shone down on the green mountains and were reflected by the lake below.

She needed the time to herself. It had been a week since the Toa delegate had visited them. Surprisingly, the world hadn't ended. There'd been no more attacks. Not yet. Labeth had gone about her day, listened to citizens' supplications, and eaten with her family and friends while generals prepared the army and drafted new men. The tension in her chest had never left.

She wanted it to all be over already and it hadn't even started. She'd grown to hate her day-to-day duties for she felt nothing meaningful was being done about the war on the horizon. That day had been so tiring as she'd been stuck in the throne room the whole time with her mother listening to citizens' supplications. It had gone on for hours, had a short break for lunch, and then had continued for hours more. While many of the issues had easy solutions, there were several for which there appeared to be none. Those were the cases that kept piling up.

Today had included the eighth complaint they had received by a farmer about a factory polluting the surrounding wildlife. The factory disposed its waste into a stream from which the farmer's animals drank, poisoning them. Labeth had felt for the farmer when he had related how so many generations of his family had worked on that farm only for it to get destroyed by the factory. However, instead of siding with the farmer, her mother had stayed neutral and added his complaint to the list that would be looked into for a better solution.

"Can we not shut down the factory?" Labeth had suggested once the supplicants had left. "We can't let it continue to pollute our streams."

"We cannot shut down that man's livelihood so easily. And we need the factory for the resources it makes," her mother had replied.

"But can he not just return to his previous occupation? We were fine before we started utilizing these new inventions, so surely we can make do without them again."

"It's not so easy to go back once things have changed."

It may not be easy, but it might be worth it, Labeth thought. All of their technologies came from trading with the Toa and had proven themselves greedy and given to the corruption of natural resources just like their inventors. In her opinion, Loreiak had been better off without anything to do with them.

She felt a pang of sadness as she remembered the woman who had lost her son. One of the meetings Labeth had been required to attend that week was with the generals as they discussed battle strategies. All of the troops would be called to mobilize in the next few weeks, Osilor among them. A draft was imminent.

And no one hears.

Labeth stroked the empty pages of her journal. How did one make them hear? How did one stop a war?

She hunted from the stars a drop of inspiration, but they burrowed into her like the thousand eyes of everyone watching her to see if she would live up to her responsibilities and their expectations. As she gazed out at the mountains, the night grew darker and the air colder. It was probably a change in the wind.

Her thoughts one by one dissipated as if washed away. She was attuned to the spreading of her lungs, of her rib cage as she breathed. The night existed around her and somehow inside her—vast, quiet, and dark. The yearning in her chest tightened and then relaxed like the letting of water as she spoke:

> "The woman's sorrow thunders in my ear.
> It beats without change and its ripple's tread
> breaks all around before it disappears.
> No one remembers, but I can't forget.
> Do they not see? Can they not hear
> the blood that drops into the water, and spreads
> as they prepare their cannons and their spears?
> What words could stop them before we're all dead?"

Labeth didn't understand how it was possible after her writer's block for the poem to flow out of her as effortless and powerful as the waterfall's descent into the river. Even at her best, she had nowhere near that skill. And the creation of it was unlike anything she had ever experienced. It was from beyond herself. The night? The stars?

Standing, she stepped closer to where the cliff gave way to the world. Her senses expanded. She could feel the velvety night sky and run her fingers through the refreshing coolness of the air. Space yawned inside her, at its center a sadness so deep it could never belong to someone as naive and sheltered as she. It had devoured centuries. Millennia. She closed her eyes and continued:

> "Beneath her flesh once lay the light I crave.
> Her pulse thudded at my fingertips, and
> I broke her neck to get my rage out. Blood
> stopped pumping—flesh and life gone to the grave.
> And I continue. I always continue, damned.
> What fate can stop me before they're all dead?"

As the moment passed, she became aware of wetness on her cheeks. Her ribcage was tight, and her hands shook. She had sweat from the delivery of the poem as if it had been a child.

Slowly, she opened her eyes.

And saw nothing but darkness.

The lake, the sky, everything gone. Even the crickets had become silent. There was no more wind. And the stench of something wrong filled everything, like a physical weight, like humidity clinging to her skin. Was she dead?

She shook the thought away for it was ridiculous.

Out of the corner of her eye, the darkness moved. It spun around her so slowly at first it had been imperceptible, but once she'd caught it, she saw it clearer and clearer. It looked like smoke. *In smoke it flies for eyes can't confine its faithful form.*

No, she wasn't dead. This was worse. She was surrounded by a Jemalgee.

Screaming, she lurched back, tripping and landing on her hip. Before she could react, she slipped over the edge of the cliff. She watched it speed further and further away, no possibility of grabbing it.

A flash of black raced to her left, and she landed on something soft. The wrongness seeped into her skin again, and when she screamed and tore at whatever she had landed on, wisps of blackness drifted through her fingers. The Jemalgee had caught her. It snaked one of its smoke tentacles around her waist. It was both strong and vaporous, an unnatural combination that made Labeth's head spin trying to comprehend it.

The Jemalgee deposited her onto the shore. She tried to scramble away but couldn't make her legs work to stand. When the creature hovered before her, she screamed anew. Eventually, her cries morphed into pleas for mercy.

Her pulse thudded at my fingertips, and I broke her neck to get my rage out.

That was what it meant to do to her. She could feel the warmth of skin over the beating of the vein so vividly, like it had spent days imagining every detail. Or had done it enough times.

"I heard someone from over here," said a voice. Footsteps approached from the forest behind her. She crawled toward them and screamed for help.

Two guards and priests approached. The search party. Various groups of guards and priests still patrolled the mountains around Soros Cereminir looking for the Jemalgee from the night of Reshelia's wedding. They froze upon seeing that they had in fact found it.

Beginning to chant a ritual, the priest poured obsidian dust in a line in front of him. Earth was the Dual of barriers, and since obsidian was the strongest, it was always the choice one for protection against Jemalgee. But the priest couldn't perform the ritual fast enough. The Jemalgee grabbed one of the guards in a smoky tentacle and threw him head first into the trunk of a large oak. The crunch of his neck made Labeth's stomach heave.

The other guard took Labeth in his arms and carried her behind the obsidian barrier. A buzzing filled the air and the priest's chanting grew louder. The obsidian dust rose in the air, and sparks of blue-white fire danced between the particles. Only the purest light could hurt a Jemalgee and give them the best chance at protection. The wall of obsidian and sparks moved to create a dome around them, but the Jemalgee smacked the priest to the side and the ritual broke.

It had reached through the shield to do it, and the white fire shot through its smoky form. It shook with flashes like lightning in a thundercloud and roared. The guard tried to take Labeth away, but she could not look away as the Jemalgee recovered and moved to kill the priest. She ran between them.

"Please." She couldn't speak higher than a whisper. She didn't know what she expected to accomplish, but she couldn't watch the priest die.

The Jemalgee paused above her. A large plume of its smoke body rose over her, blocking the stars, and its tendrils edged around her. Growing and growing.

Labeth looked into where she felt its face should be, and though it had no eyes, the weight of its attention pushed her to her knees. It sucked her in till she didn't think she could look away. "Please," she repeated. "Don't kill us."

As she stared into it, she no longer felt where her consciousness ended and its began. A depression filled the space so that even the thought of movement was beyond her. It knew all the horror it had ever caused. It would never forget any moment no matter how many millennia of memories it was forced to carry. The life it had just taken added to the constant dripping of blood reminding it that it would never change. It was the macabre version of the star it had once been—that it longed to be again. For all Jemalgee once existed as stars, the ultimate beings of light and goodness, before they were corrupted by the Ghustaugness. There was no going back. Only more blood. And no death could stop it for it and the rest of its kind were immortal. Though its actions horrified it, it was bound to reek more and more suffering. And here was this girl. Begging for mercy. It could never give itself mercy, so why should it give it to others? But it could not kill this girl.

"Depart, and don't return," it told her and disappeared into the night.

Labeth collapsed, feeling like herself again. She was panting. *It had spared them because of her.* The Jemalgee didn't spare people. Why had this one done so?

"What is going on?" said the queen as she entered in her nightgown and robe, her hair in a sleep-rumpled braid.

After rescuing her, the guard and priest had taken Labeth to a sitting room in the palace and had sent for the queen. It was near the darkest hour of the night, and the scones on the stone pillars did not provide enough light, so a fire had been lit in the hearth. It didn't warm the chill that clung to Labeth. She slipped her bare feet in-between the rugs to warm them, for she'd left her shoes—and her writing journal—on the mountain.

"We, um—," the guard lowered his head bashfully, "found the Crown Princess while on patrol."

Labeth pitied him. She wouldn't have wanted to be the one delivering that news either.

Her mother shook her by the arm. "What were you doing out there?"

The priest stepped forward. "Your Majesty, you must not—."

Someone shoved the queen away from Labeth and, reciting some words, punched Labeth in the chest. Her vision went white and her jaw locked up as a tingling sensation overwhelmed her body like nails on a chalkboard. There was a thud, and she came to. She'd fallen from her chair onto the stone floor, banging her already bruised hip.

High Priest Dlanacen stood over her, the caster of the ritual. She was really starting to not like him.

"Would you like to have your hand cut off for that?" Her mother grabbed him by the collar.

"They found her with the Jemalgee!" he cried.

Paling, her mother released him and stared horrified at Labeth.

"I had to make sure she hadn't been possessed. It could've gone into you, Your Majesty." He straightened his collar and turned to the other priest. "It should've been done before she was allowed back into the palace."

"I'm not possessed!" Labeth clumsily climbed back onto her chair and sank into it, rubbing her chest.

"We see that now," said Dlanacen.

"What. Happened?" demanded her mother.

Everyone looked at Labeth.

"I was out in the woods above the palace when I saw it—."

"Why were you out there?" her mother asked.

Labeth gulped before answering. Her chest still hurt, and it was difficult to catch her breath. "I was writing. I like being outside. It helps," she mumbled. She didn't like admitting her night escapades in front of everyone. No doubt it would get out and everyone would think her a fool.

Her mother's eyebrows rose in the perfect expression of incredulous disdain. Her only other motion was to place her hands on her hips because that stare was command enough to talk.

"It came after me, and I slipped off the cliff." She couldn't bring herself to tell of the poem they had shared. Now that her mind was clear of fright, she knew that it was the Jemalgee who had helped her create that poem. They were creatures that spoke only in poetry and could write one of the most secret parts of one's soul into one. The first eight lines had been it helping her to express that yearning she couldn't name on her own, but the last six had belonged to him. It felt wrong to admit it. To have a connection with a creature so corrupt. What did that mean for her? And she longed for it. They wouldn't understand.

"It saved me. I would've landed in the lake. It caught me and took me to the shore. And that's when they found me." With everything going on, she hadn't time to process that this creature, one whose every inclination was bound to tilt toward darkness, had rescued her from death and spared the priest at her plea. It didn't fit with anything she had been taught.

"You must find this Unfounded thing at once!" her mother ordered Dlanacen. "Tonight."

The guard nodded from the corner. "We will send more teams out at once, Your Majesty."

"No, that is not what I mean. Those have not worked. It's time to try something different," said her mother, her gaze never leaving Dlanacen.

The high priest looked to the ceiling as if it could take him away, sighed, and snapped his fingers at the other priest in the room, several ranks below him. "Phoren, come here." Phoren was a man of forty years with a widow's peak and a full, nicely trimmed beard. As he obeyed Dlanacen, he walked with hunched shoulders and fidgeting hands like a child about to be reprimanded.

Taking his shoulder, Dlanacen led him to sit on the couch across from Labeth. "Prepare a farseeking ritual. I'll get your elements."

"But sir, perhaps one of the more skilled priests could do it."

"I know your skills are adequate to the task, Phoren. And we have no time to waste." With a glance at Labeth's mother, he left.

"A farseeking ritual?" asked Labeth. It was one of the easiest to learn. It allowed the caster to send out their consciousness to find or speak with another person across great distances. "Why wasn't that tried before?"

Phoren began to whisper as he formed the poem for the ritual and didn't respond. Her mother turned her back to him. "It's a last resort," was all she said.

Dlanacen returned with a candle, a bag of obsidian, and a small mirror in the shape of a hexagon. Phoren moved to the floor so the high priest could pour a circle of obsidian dust around him, and after lighting the candle, he handed it and the mirror to him. Beginning to recite, Phoren placed the candle in front of him and tilted the hexagon in various directions. It was supposed to guide his thoughts as he sent them out. His eyes grew glassy. Labeth shrank back into her chair, for his expression reminded her of a dead fish.

Though she didn't understand why this ritual had been saved as a last resort, her skin was covered in goosebumps at the brush of premonition that something really bad was about to happen. She wanted to stop it, to say that they should leave this Jemalgee alone for it wasn't as bad as its brethren, but she didn't want to annoy her mother more. Farseeking rituals were common. They happened every single day. Possibly every hour. They weren't dangerous. But then, few had ever tried to farseek a Jemalgee.

The right side of Phoren's face twitched, and his jaw hung slack for a second. "I found it," he gasped. "It's. . ." He squinted, looking right through Labeth. She lowered her eyes to avoid his creepy stare and focused on the mirror in his hands, steady now that he had found his prey. It reflected the flames of the fire.

"It's in a cave," he continued. "Near the top of Mt. Raseynor, above even the Yaynoxce waterfall. Past the tree with branches like a crow's wings, where there are only rocks left. Turn left. You must climb the last mossy ridge to come to its tunnel." Phoren wrinkled his nose. "It's rotten, sir," he whispered, like he dare not speak louder. Like it would hear him.

"That should be enough," said Dlanacen. "You may return to us."

Phoren's body went ridged, his spine arching. He threw his head back as a strangled sound bubbled from his throat. He screamed. When Dlanacen tried to take the mirror from him, Phoren smashed it on the floor and knocked over the candle. Its flame licked at the carpet, and the guard smothered it. Phoren pressed himself against the couch, still screaming, and began knocking his head against the edge of the wooden arm. Dlanacen tried to pull him away so he wouldn't hurt himself.

"Make it stop!" Phoren cried, his sobs overcoming his screams. Each time he repeated his plea, it sounded like he lost more hope that it would ever be granted till he stopped altogether. His eyes never lost their glassiness, and his mouth hung open as he began to drool.

"Is he dead?" Labeth asked.

"No, but he is lost to us," replied Dlanacen.

"Take a large group of priests and guards to that cave now," the queen ordered the high priest. "I want it banished to the Unfound World."

"I'll round up my best men immediately, Your Majesty."

Labeth stood. "Take Phoren to the infirmary now. Make sure he receives the best treatments known in Soros Cereminir and tell his family what's happened."

Dlanacen looked at her mother for confirmation, which annoyed Labeth. Her command should be enough. When would her people stop treating her like a child?

"Do as she says," said her mother.

The guard and Dlanacen carried Phoren away. Once they were gone, her mother told her, "I'm doubling the amount of guards outside your doors. How could you be so foolish to sneak outside the palace at night? Especially with Jemalgee lurking about. You're lucky it didn't possess you."

"I'm sorry, Mother."

"Don't do it again. Now go to your room."

Labeth obeyed. She undressed and flopped onto her bed, expecting to be exhausted, but her mind wouldn't sink into sleep. She went to her windows and saw the priests head up the mountain on horseback. It was six priests in total with three guards and three chained prisoners bringing up the rear.

They were most likely murderers or perpetrators of other heinous crimes. The worst criminals were kept in the Temple District's dungeons, on reserve for moments like these—to be used as blood sacrifices. Most of Loreiak's sacrifices were done with small animals like goats, foxes, chickens, and the like. Very rarely would there be a call for a greater sacrifice, and appeasing a Jemalgee was at the top of that list. At least, Labeth assumed they would be offered as blood sacrifices. That would the luckier fate, for the other option would be to have their bodies offered as vessels for the Jemalgee to do what it willed with them, which often also ended in death or madness.

Her mother wanted it banished to the Unfound World, so the prisoners could only be a distraction or bribes in an effort to get it to comply. The thought made her chest tighten. The Unfound World was a plane that existed beneath theirs, the Found World, and was filled with all kinds of evil—spirits that would make cannibals of its hosts and sleep demons who helped the Sandman drag people down into the realm in-between the Found and Unfound Realms, possibly for forever. It was foretold that the further one got from the surface, the more dangerous it became with immortal creatures with infinite power. Some believed the Unfound World to be the source of all Ghustaugness. Rarely did anyone or anything come back from it. That's why Loreiak had taken to banishing the Jemalgee there. It was the only place that could hold them. But there were stories that since they were closer to the Ghustaugness there, the Jemalgee grew even more corrupt.

Labeth grabbed some spare paper from her desk and wrote down the poem she and the Jemalgee had created. In the quiet night, she whispered it back to herself. It was beautiful. The poem expressed her frustrations with the fickleness of the world so well. She scanned the last six lines.

Her pulse thudded at my fingertips, and I broke her neck to get my rage out. The description hadn't been of what it had intended to do to Labeth like she assumed, but was a memory of what it had already done. *And I continue. I always continue, damned. What fate can stop me before they're all dead?*

These weren't the words of a monster bent on evil, but a creature helpless to stop its own corruption no matter how much it desired it. Just as she wished to stop the war and end the sorrows of her kingdom. But this was also the creature that had possessed one of the women at the bar and had killed the other. Labeth touched her neck, shuddering at the memory.

It's evil, she reminded herself. It killed a man in front of you and almost killed you.

But the reminders couldn't shake what her soul felt to be true. This Jemalgee was different, and he—for something about its voice had seemed male--had known her in a way impossible for any other creature. They had connected. She wanted to see him again.

But it was best to stay away. She closed her journal and went back to bed.

III

WHEN RESHELIA AND HITHLIN ENTERED the dining room, Labeth knew something was off. For their first month as a married couple, they had spent it vacationing in the Northern Castle. This was the first time Labeth had seen them since. The royal family always had dinner together, and though Hithlin had attended a few as Reshelia's betrothed, this would be his first time as an official member of the family.

Labeth embraced Reshelia and asked how she was.

"The Northern Castle was lovely," was all she said. Labeth waited an awkward moment for her to go on because surely her sister had more to say about her honeymoon—about being married, the thing of her dreams. But nothing more came.

The family settled around the stone table. The dining room was an oval that jutted out of the side of the palace halfway. The side facing the exterior was covered in vibrant colored stained glass. The setting sun made the blues, reds, golds, and purples glow an even deeper hue. The stone table was incredibly thick, as if the builders had intended to make it too heavy to be moved, therefore ensuring the royal family would use it for centuries. Its sides were plated in gold and silver. A candelabrum stood in the center over two large, juicy chickens, steamed vegetables, and sweet bread.

The conversation started out stilted for a family reunion. Hithlin and the queen carried most of it. Labeth was too concerned with figuring out what was wrong, and Asanilph seemed uninterested. It didn't come together till the queen asked Hithlin if he had spoken with the generals.

"Yes," he replied. "I am very grateful to be commanding my own fleet of ships. General Teyth briefed me on the mission as soon as we had returned."

"Do you think you can leave next week?"

"So soon?" said Labeth, her appetite vanished. Osilor had just left to join the army on the eastern coast a week ago, and Labeth had been busy trying to comfort Josa despite all of her words of reassurance tasting hollow. She couldn't promise anyone would be okay.

"Of course, Your Majesty," said Hithlin. "I would do anything for our country and your family." He glanced at Reshelia, taking her hand and squeezing it.

"I'm pregnant," she blurted out.

The table went silent.

"You two wasted no time," Asanilph joked but no one laughed.

Labeth hurried to the other side of the table and knelt in front of Reshelia, taking her other hand. "I'm so sorry."

"He has to protect our country so our child can have a good life," she replied, turning to her husband like she was asking for reassurance from him rather than proclaiming what she truly believed.

"It is a sad reality," said their mother, her eyes downcast. She looked more tired than Labeth had ever seen her. "But there have always been battles we've had to fight for our family and there always will be. And we are still standing and your child will stand with us."

As Reshelia slipped her hand out of Labeth's to take their mother's, Labeth looked to Hithlin. He was such a good man. Didn't complain about anything he'd had to deal with but always celebrated the good he had gained. Labeth was confident he would be a good husband to Reshelia and he would be a great father.

A week later, they said goodbye to him. Since the Toa had attacked several cities along the Toun cliffs to the east, a fleet needed to be sent out as soon as possible in response. It would all be under Hithlin's command, and *The Silver Snake* would be his own. The day he left, they traveled to the town Ilsaphanor on the southern coast to see him off. A great crowd of common folk, courtiers, priests, and the royal family threw colored powder representing protection on the soldiers as they passed through the streets toward the docks. By the time they reached their ships, they were covered in a tie-dye of green, red, blue, pink, and gold. Too many of them were so young.

The people cheered them on with confidence and hope, but nothing could mask the solemnity of the departing. Labeth knew the rumors, the fears whispered between families and friends at night. That Loreiak soldiers, no matter how numerous, couldn't match the technological superiority of the Toa.

Labeth had to hold onto her hope. She hugged her sister as they said goodbye to her husband.

Three months later, he was dead.

Labeth finished tying the silver ribbon on the bouquet of pansies she had gathered. The flowers were a collection of white, purple, pink, and orange that she had picked from the palace's gardens. She hoped Reshelia would like it.

It was an overcast day, grimy with humidity. Thankfully, it wasn't raining yet, but she could smell it coming. Pulling her maroon cloak tighter around her, she headed back toward the palace.

It had been a month since news of Hithlin's death had come to the palace. *The Silver Snake* had been sunk by a submarine. They'd had no chance. They hadn't seen their opponent. Not all of the fleet had been destroyed, but *The Silver Snake* and its captain had been lost to the sea. They hadn't even had his body for the funeral.

A sob escaped her throat, and she pressed her handkerchief to her mouth as she passed the guards to the entrance of the palace. They gave her solemn nods, their eyes downcast and likewise dejected. Talk of the war was everywhere. A new attack, a new death, what would happen next?

A servant moved to walk in front of her with a lantern. Black drapes hung over all the windows, so it was dark even in the middle of the day. As they ascended the spiral stairs up to the northwest tower, Labeth was tempted to pull the drapes down. They hid beautiful stained glass windows twice her height.

Asanilph sat inside Reshelia's bed chambers when Labeth arrived. An older woman bustled around the bedroom—a mystic healer by the name of Sorsetha. Her skin was tan and weathered, and she always wore decorative pins in her hair and tassels from her ears. Though she liked brightly patterned dresses, lately she wore black ones out of respect. Labeth had known her since she was a child, for she always loved to scare the children with stories about mystic creatures—the Jemalgee included—like kooky, older women tended to do.

Labeth handed Sorsetha the bouquet. "Can you put these somewhere Reshelia will like?"

"Of course." She smiled, admiring the flowers, and left to find a vase.

Labeth reluctantly turned toward the bed. Asanilph sat on the edge, holding Reshelia's hand. Reshelia stared straight through Labeth, her blue eyes unfocused and still like Phoren after he had farseeked the Jemalgee. He had never recovered. Though her hair had been combed, she wasn't wearing make-up like she usually did, and the lack of it and any sign of emotion made Reshelia look sick and frail. She had been in this stupor since Hithlin's death and hadn't spoken a word or gotten out of bed. She hardly moved, and the servants had to force her to eat and drink.

Sitting on the other side of the bed, Labeth took Reshelia's hand. It was cold. Was she dead? Labeth checked to see that her chest rose and fell. It did, but none of her anxiety left her.

"Has there been any change?" Labeth asked Asanilph. She knew the answer but it seemed a ritual that had to be done every day. What else was there to say? As she stared at her sister's empty face, Labeth's sadness bloomed into hot anger. "I wish we could go back to before any of this happened. And those blasted people would stop attacking us. What do they think they're gaining with all this bloodshed? It's such a cruel waste of life."

"They want our magic," said Sorsetha, who had returned with the pansies in a vase. "They've always been jealous that their section doesn't have it."

Her sister would have to suffer for a nation's greed. So did the woman she had met in the bar, mourning her dead son. Hithlin was gone forever. And so would many more people. With all the power afforded to her position of crown princess, she was powerless to stop it, merely a cog in a world full of people and their greedy wills.

"Is there something we could do to wake her, Sorsetha?" asked Asanilph.

"I fear not." The woman refilled Reshelia's bedside lamp with oil. "Her grief has captured her spirit and will only release it through the spilling of tears. She cannot return to us till she cries, and as long as she doesn't, she'll remain in this state."

"Couldn't we just put an onion underneath her nose?" asked Asanilph, and Labeth snorted despite herself.

Sorsetha gave her a look, but her irritation wasn't serious. "No. That would not work. Onions cannot bring forth a spirit." She brushed some hair to the side of Reshelia's face. "She needs to get better soon. It's not good for the baby." She left.

Labeth stroked the small bump on Reshelia's belly, mostly camouflaged by the heavy blankets. She couldn't feel any movement. She didn't know if that was normal at this point or not. It was a miracle she hadn't miscarried already, and there was no way the baby would survive while her mother was barely alive.

"I think the onions would be worth a shot," said Asanilph with a shrug. "Labeth?"

Sorsetha's words had triggered something in Labeth so that she missed her sister's words. She mumbled, "We need something to bring forth her spirit." She looked to her youngest sister. "I have an idea." She didn't speak with pride or excitement but fear. It was a crazy idea. And she'd have to disobey her mother to do it.

"What?" asked Asanilph, sensing that this plan was not going to be as simple as chopping an onion.

"We need. . . a Jemalgee."

"Okay, I'll tell Mother you've gone insane." When Asanilph moved to rise, Labeth grabbed her arm to keep her sitting.

"A Jemalgee is the only creature that can read a person's soul." She lowered her voice even though there was no one to hear them. It had been five months since the incident with the Jemalgee. The priests had tried to banish him to the Unfound World but they had found nothing in the cave when they had arrived.

And there'd been no sighting of any Jemalgee around Soros Cereminir since.

Labeth had tried her best to move on though he filled her
thoughts more nights than not. Though she'd been tempted, she
hadn't sneaked out to her favorite writing spot because she wanted to prove to her mother that she was taking her duties serious-
ly. It was a crazy idea to suggest contacting a Jemalgee and would
definitely cause her to lose all of the respect she'd gained from her
mother if anyone were to find out. But if the Jemalgee could save
Reshelia, it would be worth it.

"The first time I met the one, he helped me write a poem.
Everything I'd been struggling to say, or even to comprehend, he
drew it out of me and put it in the most beautiful words. That's
what Reshelia needs to process her grief. He can draw her spirit
out of her."

"And how do you expect to find him? Or convince him to
help us?"

"I know you've been practicing mysticism."

"How?"

"You got chalk on my shoes the night of Reshelia's wedding.
Or were you too drunk to remember?" Chalk was the most common means for creating a barrier when practicing rituals. And
Asanilph didn't seem the type to be into acrobatics or children
sidewalk games.

"I remember," said Asanilph a bit too vehemently. "Sorsetha's
been teaching me. She's promised to not tell anyone. Don't tell
Mother."

"Do you think I want her to know I've spoken to a Jemalgee again?"

"Oh, yeah," said Asanilph with a sly smile. "Mother might lock you in the dungeons for that. Are you willing to risk it?"

"I'm not letting Reshelia waste away if there's something I can do about it. We can tell Mother she got better on her own."

Asanilph shook her head with an incredulous smile, rubbing her forehead. "And how in the Unfound World will you convince a Jemalgee to help us? And not possess us or kill us?"

"He won't do that to me. I don't know why, but we have a connection. I'm not sure if he'll help us, but I have to try. Will you help me find him?"

Asanilph looked for a long moment at Reshelia. Usually, it was Reshelia who dominated conversations with her exuberance. Labeth knew that it pained Asanilph just as much as it did her to see their sister reduced to the ash of what she really was.

"Fine," agreed Asanilph.

That night, Labeth and Asanilph declared they would be staying in Reshelia's room to keep her company, so they could cast the ritual to find the Jemalgee. It would be a farseeking ritual, just like the one Phoren had cast. Touching the Jemalgee's mind with his had driven the priest mad. Doing this could break her. But her gut said that the Jemalgee wouldn't hurt her. That they had a connection. He had the chance to hurt her but had let her go for some reason. And a catatonic Reshelia watching over them from her bed made the choice easy.

As Labeth lit the candle between them, Asanilph asked, "Are you sure this is a good idea?"

"It'll be fine, I promise." Labeth blew the match out and grabbed the small makeup mirror she'd taken from her dressing table.

"I'm not sure if I can read far enough to find him. He could be all the way to the Northern Castle."

"He could. But we have to try. And with both us, we'll be able to farseek farther. So how do we do this?"

"We'll recite the ritual together, and since you know who we're looking for, you'll be the one to tilt the mirror to direct the light wherever you want to farseek. I'll just be here to give you energy and help control it since you don't know what you're do-ing." Labeth let the jab fall off her. She was too nervous to give a witty comeback.

"Let's do it then." Labeth placed her right hand in her sisters left and steered the mirror with her other one. They recited:

> "Mirror, guide this light for us. See
> what we seek—one
> that all have shunned.
> Find him so we may give our plea."

Labeth's sight detached from her physical form as the ritual channeled her consciousness in the direction she chose. It was like flying like a bird but faster than any creature she knew of. She could soar among the clouds or dive through the dirtiest tunnels of the city as low as the rats. She wisped through windowpanes.

She could see so much. It was dizzying. She was tempted to touch some of the city dwellers in their sleep. Could she know their dreams? Since she'd not been trained in mysticism, she knew little of the extent of the magic's reach—an oversight.

She drew back from them. No, she had to focus on her mission. But how would she find him?

She remembered how it felt when they had touched souls. Now that she was seeking him, her desire to feel that connection again awoke like hunger pains. When he gazed into her, she was known—something she had always longed for but could never seem to get.

She drifted in another direction, no longer fully in control. She let whatever it was pull her, faster and faster till everything blurred, and she stopped in a room with fancy furnishings, thick rugs, and tapestries draped everywhere. Since there were no windows and only a couple of lanterns on the walls, the room was dark in a homey way. On all of Labeth's sides were golden bars, and the air was scratched and smudged in places before her. She was looking out from a mirror.

On the couch with his back turned to her was a man with dark hair. Though Labeth remained silent, he stirred and turned to look at her. It was him. As he rose from the couch, a woman moaned. There was someone with him, but she remained asleep.

He approached with a stony expression. He wore a velvet robe that was loose over the chest. Around his neck draped thin gold chains, and jewels decorated his ears. Obviously, it couldn't be his body. He'd possessed this man to use him for his own pleasure. Labeth glanced around the room, wondering what sort of things he was up to in a place like this. It disgusted her to see him use another person like that, and she couldn't help but to imagine what it felt like for a Jemalgee to crawl into her skin and rape her of her freewill.

"Why are you here?" he asked.

"I...I..." Now that she was before him, the whole plan seemed ridiculous. She should go. He would yell at her, threaten her.

But he stayed silent. Staring. She fidgeted under his gaze.

"My sister cannot escape her grief over her husband's death. She lies in bed all day without moving, without eating or drinking or saying anything. She's wasting away, and we haven't been able to get her out of it. And she's pregnant," Labeth added softly. "She needs to finally express her grief so her spirit can come forward and she can move on." She hesitated. Here it was. "You have the power to read a person's soul. Could you draw her spirit out?"

He took a step back as if she was the one to fear. It took her a while to realize that it wasn't disgust or anger on his face that she would dare ask him for anything, but horror at the nature of her request. "You do not know the thing you ask for."

"You're right. I don't understand a lot of this. But I'm desperate," she replied. This was the only hope she had and dammit, she would sink her nails into it. "My sister and the baby will die if this goes on any longer. Please. If you can do anything, help us."

"It's possible, but rarely have I given good with it—more madness from mirrored truth to bring them deeper into darkness, not out."

"That's not true. That night on the lake, you drew that poem out of me and you didn't drive me mad." Labeth hesitated for she had never admitted this next part aloud. "It was beautiful. And I knew your heart too. You want to do good. Why run away from the chance?"

"Every time I've tried it's brought disaster!" He turned away. "Go back and never seek me out again. For your own good."

Labeth called for him to wait, but when she tried to go after him, the mirror held her inside. She slapped her palms against the glass. "Please, I can't let my sister die! I know you can do this. There is good in you. I've seen it."

He stopped retreating, his back still turned to her. A long moment passed.

"You've seen it?" he asked.

It no longer mattered to her what everyone said for she knew what she had sensed. He had saved her life and shown her mercy when she'd stepped between him and the priest. And that poem they had shared had come straight from his soul. Both of them longed to stop what was evil in the world from winning as it so often seemed to do but also shared the same sense of helplessness. But Labeth wouldn't accept that. There was a way to stop it all. There had to be. And it started with healing her sister. "Yes," she told him with as much conviction as she could muster.

He turned his head slightly so she could see his profile. "I will help you."

It was the first time in months that Labeth had been outside the palace for any reason other than offering sacrifices in the Temple District. She was giddy with excitement to be out on the streets, among her people, free again. Well, not exactly free, she thought. Asanilph walked beside her, Labeth pushed Reshelia in a wheelchair, and nine guards walked around them. She hadn't been able to sneak out in disguise like she had during Reshelia's wedding because of the careful watch her mother continued to hold on her after her first encounter with the Jemalgee. But also, it would've been nearly impossible to explain the disappearances of all three princesses for one afternoon. Labeth rolled her eyes at the extravagance. The guards weren't even there to protect the princesses as much as they were to keep them from running off. After these past months of obedience, her mother still did not trust her. Labeth couldn't be too annoyed though, because she was right not to.

It'd been three days since she and Asanilph had contacted the Jemalgee. He could not read Reshelia's soul from a distance so they had to meet in person, and he could not enter the palace grounds because of the protection spells the priests had cast. It had been Asanilph's idea that they meet at the mystic healer Sorsetha's place in the city, under the guise of wanting to take Reshelia to soak in one of her special baths.

Labeth stood on tiptoe to peek over the guards' shoulders. They blocked her view of almost everything. The streets were not as busy as normal, and there was a significant lack of young men around. Many had already been drafted for the war. Everything seemed drearier, more run down. Labeth wasn't sure if it was just her imagination or the effect of the cloudy sky or that her country was hurting. The war was only a few months old and already the people's morale seemed dampened though they flew Loreiak's flag from every shop window and balcony. How much longer can this go on, she thought. Everyday, the future became bleaker and bleaker.

Sorsetha's shop was a short, wooden building in a market square down near Lake Urvuspha. The front of the shop was cramped full of shelves with ingredients for rituals and other trinkets believed to hold special mystical properties. There were necklaces of protection, fabrics that could help promote fertility or strength when worn, and mirrors. Tons of small mirrors of various shapes hung together on strings dangling from the ceiling. They twisted around and clinked against each other like wind chimes at the slightest breeze. Other than the ingredients and mirrors, most of the trinkets were full of superstition and had no real power.

When they entered, Sorsetha embraced Labeth and Asanilph. "I received a message a couple of hours ago that you were coming. I've already prepared a concoction for her bath."

"Thank you so much for all you've done, Sorsetha," said Labeth. The woman was so earnest in her desire to help them that Labeth felt guilty about using her kindness and her shop to meet with the Jemalgee.

"I only wish I could do more." She squeezed Reshelia's hand, her smile slipping, replaced with pity.

She led the princesses into the back of the shop, away from the guards. They would have to wait while the princesses bathed their sister, giving them the privacy they needed for their plan. In one of the back rooms, a servant girl poured hot water into a bath set in the ground. The bath itself was made out of rocks and mud so the bather could soak in their natural minerals. When the servant girl moved to undress Reshelia, Labeth held up her hand. "We will do it ourselves."

"As you wish, Your Highness," said Sorsetha. She and the servant girl left them.

Once alone, Labeth and Asanilph undressed Reshelia, lowered her into the tub, and poured the concoction into it. Even though it had not been the reason why they had come, Labeth saw no point in not trying. Maybe it would help to draw Reshelia out of her stupor and they wouldn't need the Jemalgee after all.

As they washed her hair, Asanilph asked, "When is it going to get here?"

"I told him we would be here two hours after noon. He should arrive soon."

Looking around everywhere, Asanilph washed and combed the same lock of Reshelia's hair several times over, betraying her nervousness. "What if it doesn't come?"

Labeth sighed. She'd been blocking that question from her mind as best she could. She wanted to snap at Asanilph to not say such things. She had too much depending on this. Instead, she ran the back of her finger over Reshelia's temple and cheek. With her skin against her sister's, it was more obvious how pale and sickly Reshelia had become. The fat in her cheeks had disappeared, and as she and Asanilph had lowered her into the tub, Labeth had seen how much weight she'd lost. Her body was thin and bony except for her slightly swollen belly.

"He'll come." He has too.

They washed and combed Reshelia's hair till there was a knock on the other door in the room, the one leading outside that the servants used when carrying in water. Gasping, Asanilph turned to Labeth with fear in her eyes. Her youngest sister was usually so brazen, cocky really, that it set Labeth's nerves on edge to see her afraid. She gritted her teeth. He would not hurt them, she reminded herself. She rose and opened the door.

Outside was a boy of ten or eleven years. He barely reached the height of Labeth's shoulders. His arms and legs were skinny, and there was still much baby fat on his face. Too much for him to be looking so hard as he stared at her with the eyes of a Jemalgee.

When she cringed in disgust, the Jemalgee lowered the boy's head. "Do you wish for me to see her still?" he said quietly.

Labeth blushed for she hadn't meant to react that way. Since she knew how much he hated his cursed self, she felt bad for making him feel ashamed, but taking the host of a young boy wasn't right. Taking any host wasn't.

"Yes, come in." She stepped aside for him.

When he entered, Asanilph backed away against the far wall, the white of her eyes fully visible. The Jemalgee paid her no mind. He only watched Reshelia as he strode around the tub to kneel beside her, his confident way of movement clashing with his young host. For a long moment, he stared at her, and Reshelia remained unmoving, not even noticing the Jemalgee. It was deathly silent.

Then, the Jemalgee began to sing, speaking Reshelia's feelings.

"I am a bride waiting in a bed of cobwebs.

I have no flesh nor blood for I am empty
except for a child who will know no father
and a skeleton for a mother,
neither of whom should have been born
if death were their destinies.

My love was warm and sweet
with strength to support
the bridge of our hearts from crumbling
under catastrophe. Now I am broken,
and my love is cold and gone."

It was incredibly rare to hear a Jemalgee's voice—and to live to tell the tale, but that didn't stop there from being a plethora of accounts describing its beauty. Chilling. Otherworldly. An elixir of ecstasy and terror. A voice that can tear thy soul, milk out your deepest fears, thoughts, desires, and sorrows and make you drink them. None of these words were enough. None ever would be.

Labeth only knew that it was genderless and so pure there was no way a human body could produce such a sound. She felt tense. She couldn't move. She didn't think she blinked even as she cried. While the Jemalgee sang of her sister's grief, she saw Reshelia more intimately than she had known anyone before. Her sister's burdens were hers. Every part of them.

"My love is cold and gone,
leaving a broken half behind.
I carry his flesh and blood,

and one day she will cry Mother,
but never Father.

I don't know how to go on.
I don't know how to go on."

As the Jemalgee finished the song, Reshelia's expression shifted—just a small furrow of her brows that Labeth would've missed if it hadn't been the first time her face had changed in weeks. Then, her lips quivered, her eyes scrunched up, and she let out a wail.

Sobbing, Labeth jumped into the tub and wrapped Reshelia in her arms. Her sister's face was covered in tears, and her body shook against Labeth with life. Painful but beautiful life. Asanilph, kneeling by the tub, hugged both of them, crying as well. It was a miracle. More than that—a sign of hope she'd been craving ever since the beginning of the war and Hithlin's death. This was proof that all was not lost and that she could heal things.

She looked up to thank the Jemalgee but he was already gone.

I WAITED FOR YOU WHERE WE FIRST MET, hoping you would come but knowing it was the best that you didn't. I had left immediately after helping your sister because I didn't want you to thank me. One good deed does not bring me out of the mire of my evil to reach the level of someone who is worthy of thanks.

As I sensed you coming, I hid in the darkness of the mountain. I held myself back from speaking with you that time at least.

You were carrying a lantern and nothing to write with. From your cloak's pocket, you pulled a piece of paper and a single candle in its holder that you lit with your lantern. Kneeling on the rock, you placed the note underneath the candle and looked out into the night. I shrunk back instinctively though there was no way you could see me.

You began to speak what was on the paper—a poem for me. You couldn't know that I was there but for some reason spoke to the night's darkness anyway.

"I've heard the tales of you: your kind meanders
through bodies, kissing pleasure, giving madness.
You grow in others what you surrendered
to long ago, the Devouring Darkness.
And yet, you saved me and my sister. I
cannot repay the hope you've given me.
I hear you whenever she speaks 'cause life

has come back to her, thanks to you, Jemalgee.
You said you're damned but you've defied the role
they've bound you to. There's light in you, Creature
of Darkness. Don't forget that. Now, your soul
may shine so dimly, but I wish this lantern
will comfort you, and may you know ten times
the hope you gave when you watch its flame."

You held the candle aloft so its flame shone, a lone star, in the darkness. But I didn't watch it. I watched you for you were my star that night. My hope that I carried with me—foolishly—to the end.

Dior

WHEN THAT GIRL FARSEEKED YOU through the mirror, I awoke the second you left me to speak with her. The absence of your touch was enough to rouse me. I stayed silent and listened. It was a young girl's voice. Human, no trace of Jemalgee in her. Is this what you were keeping from me? You had disappeared after that night with the twins like you always did after one of your existential fits. You always slunk off to some cave and ignored me for a time. Still, I always led you out of them.

(Till you found the one I could not free you from).

You were different after this specific sabbatical. You wouldn't talk to me about it.

I heard her say there was good in you, and you believed her. I can't say I was surprised. You were always the dreamer. Yes, she spoke earnestly, but she's a fool—a dreamer also who sees what she wants. I deduced that from the first hope-dripping words she spoke. There is no good in us. We left that in the sky. This pursuit of redemption will break your heart. It's better to accept your fate than to foolishly believe you can be more. Weren't you tired of hoping, breaking, and crawling back into your caves only to return to my arms?

Later, I eavesdropped on you singing of the girl's sister's grief. It was so disgusting I almost rushed in to stop you (but I knew you would be mad). They don't deserve your voice! I'd cut off their ears if you would let me. . . .

Looking back, I should have stopped you. I didn't think that your silly experiment would've worked, but it did, unfortunately for you. I tried to keep you by my side, to make you see reality, but once that hope infected you, you were gone to me. That was the real beginning of the end. Not when the girl suggested her plan to save you. Not after what I did. Nor the blood that came after. The taste of healing over destruction made you love-struck blind, so blind that you forgot how the dreams of this world had seemed so pure before our damnation.

IV

Two weeks passed before Labeth saw the Jemalgee again. She'd done what was good and hadn't sought him out other than when she'd placed a candle at their first meeting as a thank you. She'd been tempted to farseek him but had reminded herself that her duty was to her kingdom. This thing—whatever it was—with the Jemalgee was a distraction. But this time he sought her out, something desperate and pleading in the eyes of the host he wore. He seemed a drowning man looking at her for hope. How could she deny him a conversation?

She was perusing shops with Josa, both wearing common clothes and personas. Labeth's mother had eased her careful watch over her when Reshelia'd awoken from her catatonia. When Labeth and Asanilph had taken their sister to see her, it was the first time Labeth had seen the queen cry. She'd hugged Reshelia like she would disappear if she loosened her grip and had kissed her face and stroked her hair and shoulders. When she asked how it had happened, the sisters told her that it'd been Sorsetha's healing baths that had done the trick. They couldn't tell the truth, for even though it had given great results, everyone would chastise them for being so foolish as to summon a Jemalgee. Reshelia did talk to her sisters about their methods. Though she'd risen from her stupor, she remained shaken and quieter than usual.

Labeth hadn't intended to test her new boundaries—other than sneaking to her favorite writing spot that one night—but Josa insisted that they do something fun, get out of that dreary castle and forget the weight of current events. Labeth had finally given into her nagging, joking that she would do it only if Josa never read Osilor's letter from war to her again. But truthfully, she had missed her secret adventures with her friend and that had been convincing enough.

They came to one shop selling scarves, cloaks, and cheap jewelry. Its front opened to the street, and that's when she saw him. He wore the host of a young woman, possibly Labeth's age, with black hair and round, blue eyes. He wore a scarf over his head and stood in the shadows like he wanted to disappear into them. He must be most comfortable there.

As Josa ventured deeper into the shop, Labeth called to her that she would be looking at the wares outside. Josa only hummed in response as she admired a necklace, and Labeth slipped across the street to the Jemalgee.

"What are you doing here?" she asked. It sounded too rude after she had said it, but she'd been so surprised.

"How's your sister?" That shocked her more. That he would care at all.

"She's well. Thank you," she replied, keeping her eyes down toward the ground.

There was a pause. "I know you do not like it when I wear a host, but it's the only way to speak with you," he said. "Since you've not returned." Labeth met his eyes, taken aback that he'd seen through her to her discomfort. Of course, he'd sensed it. He was a Jemalgee.

"You've been waiting for me. At the waterfall?" She had hoped he'd been there the night she'd gone but suspected it was far-fetched that he would take any more interest in meeting with her. It warmed her to know that she'd been wrong.

"The candle and the poem were more beautiful than anything ever offered to me. You have a gift."

"Oh, you don't have to flatter me."

"It's not flattery. Your eyes," he said, "are wonderful, not for being seen but for what they see. Light in the darkest of places."

She lowered her eyes again, this time from self-consciousness rather than disgust. He was too kind. A Jemalgee! What was this? "I have to. See the light," she added. "The world is always so dim. Poverty, disease, wars." Around them, the shops and streets were uncharacteristically sparse, the men having been shipped out and fewer goods being shipped in due to trade issues because of the war. "I feel its weight, and I have to hope that the good will prevail. Otherwise, I'd go mad." She laughed under her breath, not sure why.

"What's troubling you?"

"Do you not know of the war?"

He looked at her blankly and tilted his head as if he were trying to think back but it was difficult. "It's been in a few minds I've walked in."

Labeth ignored his mention of other hosts. "I have to believe we'll win. Loreiak has to win."

"I have seen kingdoms come and rename this valley, these hills many times. It is the way of things."

"But this is *my* country. These are *my* hills," she said, angry that he would say anything different.

"They are not. You will lose them one day, if not in war, at least in death." He lowered his gaze. "I don't mean to upset you, but to show you how pointless it all is."

"It's not pointless to me. Hithlin died for this country. My sister is pregnant, and if the Toa conquer us, they'll kill her. They'll kill me and destroy this city—the bakery on the corner of Taxoro Street, all the dancing squares, the temples, and the children will have the beliefs and traditions of their ancestors burned before them."

"I envy you." He smiled ruefully. "Once I had a heart big enough to care for all the little that you see. Don't trade it for anything." Labeth didn't know if it was another spark across the connection between them or the beauty of the eyes he stole, but his regret was palpable. She wondered how terrible it must be to see his home in the stars every night with no ability to ever return.

Exiting the store, Josa called Labeth's name and scanned the crowd. "I have to go," said Labeth. But as she pulled away, the Jemalgee grabbed her arm with a grip as strong as a chain's.

"Please visit me. I will be in the cave on top of Mt. Resaynor. Every night."

"Okay, okay," she promised, caught off guard by his urgency and her need to get back before Josa saw them.

He released her, and she returned to her friend but her mind wasn't in the present for the rest of the day. He wouldn't leave her thoughts. She pitied him for his hopeless situation and then thought, was it hopeless? Or could he be redeemed?

She hadn't been able to sneak out that night, but the opportunity came the night after. It would've been faster with a horse, but that would've drawn attention, so she hiked up the mountain on foot. Reaching her writing spot was easy, but she had never ventured further. The path narrowed and steepened with random depressions that made the way jarring.

Almost an hour passed before she saw the tree with branches like a crow's wings, just like Phoren had described. It was a gray, shriveled thing, hunched in an alcove created by two steep boulders. At the top of its trunk was a knot that looked vaguely like a bird's head, and its two curved branches flayed out to either side with several of their arms and fingers facing toward the ground like feathers.

Past the tree, the vegetation grew scarce. The lack of foliage allowed her to see the cave. Its black maw cut an impenetrable wall of blackness in the side of the mountain. Was he watching her?

She continued, having to scramble up boulders to reach the ledge in front of the cave. Above her were the stars, behind her a steep drop no one could survive, and before her the thing most feared was worse than death. She held her lantern aloft, but it didn't illuminate any of the cave's interior, as if the darkness refused to shy away from the light.

"Hello?" she called. What if he wasn't there? What if this had been some trick to make her look foolish?

The darkness of the cave shifted, and she felt his presence like a hand on her cheek, soft and cold. Tentacles of smoke slithered out along the cave's opening as a large column of smoke emerged and reared its head over her like a snake. Now that she could get a good look at him in this form, she saw that the black smoke of him constantly shifted. It ran along his body like a continuous waterfall with no clear beginning or end.

His wrongness hit her like a terrible stench. She broke out into gooseflesh. But amid that feeling was sorrow, drawing her in like a melody's pull. It was pure hopelessness.

Not sure what to do, Labeth began to bow but he stopped her. "I'm not worthy of any respect so drop the formality."

"Why did you want me to come here?"

The tower of smoke lowered, dissolving as he spread around her along the cliff's ledge. "Your presence is soothing to me. Speak."

Blushing, she sat down. "About what?"

"Anything."

So she told him about what she and Josa had done after seeing him in the marketplace. They'd stumbled upon a wedding dressmaker's shop. How Josa convinced herself—while speaking aloud to Labeth—that there was no shame in trying a couple on. Just to see what style she might like. She and Osilor had officially become engaged before he'd been deployed, but there was no date for the wedding. It could be a couple of months. It could be years. It could be never. Then Labeth told him that she thought Josa wanted to try on the dresses to assure herself that she could get to wear one. That Osilor wouldn't die. Labeth hadn't wanted to deny her that.

She mentioned how the queen had cried when she'd seen Reshelia healed and had hugged all of her daughters. How Reshelia still didn't like to talk about what she'd been through and Labeth struggled to help her.

"I'm sure your presence soothes her like it does me," he said.

"I hope so." She'd taken to playing with the thin layer of dust and pebbles over the rocky ground. When she looked up at him, she noticed how bright the stars and moon had become. It was deep into the night, so the stars were at their brightest and most plentiful. What must it have been like to be among them, looking down at the world? "Do you ever wish to return to the sky?"

"Every second, but it's impossible," he said, the pain evident in his voice.

"Have you tried?"

"I've pleaded with the stars but they have never answered my call, nor will they ever. I chose to leave, so on this earth I will stay."

"But what if there was a way to go back? Would you do it?"

"I'd do anything to be among them again. If bliss were a drink, you're drowning in it up there, as them."

"That sounds wonderful." What Labeth would give to know no trouble nor pain, only the serenity that comes with being exactly as you're supposed to be.

"But I'll never know it again," he added.

"Hey." Crawling forward, she reached into his smoke form and felt him flow over her fingers like a weird combination of water and spiderwebs. Instinct told her to shrink back, but she stayed firm. "You told me that I see light in the darkest of places. And I see it in you. You're different than the rest of them. *There's light in you, Creature of Darkness,*" she sang. "And if there is any light, then it can grow."

He withdrew from her. "If there is light, then it can be consumed."

"I won't let you give up hope."

"Why?"

"Because you restored mine," she said, remembering how the life had reignited in Reshelia's eyes at his song.

There was a long silence as all the smoke tendrils of his body crept back into the cave one by one. "Go and sleep. The night is getting deep."

"I'll come back." Again there was a long silence, and Labeth feared he might order her to never return.

"Then I'll await your rise, my evening star."

"Your Highness!"

Labeth startled awake, not sure where she was as a woman ran over to a wardrobe and started pulling out clothes. She was back in her bedroom, but she couldn't quite remember returning last night. It had been in the early morning, so she hadn't gotten much sleep.

"I didn't realize you had gone back to sleep," her maidservant said. "You're late for the meeting with the Queen and her advisors."

Sitting up to lean against her headboard, Labeth rubbed her eyes. She began to recall her maidservant dutifully waking her up earlier to get ready, but Labeth having been so tired from her late night excursion had fallen back asleep. Her mother would be furious. She wasn't awake enough to care yet.

She and her maidservant hurried to get her dressed and then left for the meeting. She grabbed a cold pastry to eat on the way. It wasn't dignified for the crown princess to do so, but she was starving. Wiping the sugar off her mouth, Labeth entered the meeting room as quietly and inconspicuously as she could, which meant knocking over a candelabrum. She'd been so focused on not disturbing the meeting that she'd neglected watching where she was going. Everyone turned to her, and her mother's brow furrowed into those familiar lines of disappointment. She silently repeated a thousand curses upon herself. May she be damned. She probably was already if her mother had anything to say about it. The meeting resumed, and Labeth stayed in the back, focusing on containing her embarrassment.

"We need to dispatch troops to take Resenmir back," said one of the advisors. "If the city stays occupied, they'll soon be able to take control of our inland infrastructure and cut off supplies to our troops on the east coast. We have to act now before it gets any worse."

Take Resenmir back. Stays occupied. That snapped Labeth out of her morning fog. What were they talking about? Looking at the others in the room, she realized that they weren't advisors. They were generals and one priest was present. This was a war meeting. Had a city been taken by the Toa? They'd been sinking ships and wreaking havoc on the coast for months but this would be the first of them invading the land, and staying.

Listening intently, Labeth discovered that the siege of the city had happened almost a full week ago, but a messenger had just reached Soros Cereminir the previous night. The generals were discussing whether they should retaliate immediately or hold back.

"We can't be sure that we could successfully take the city back at this time," said one general. "Who knows what land weapons they have that we don't know of. We should send troops to focus on protecting the roads themselves," he added pointing to the roads which ran along the eastern side of the map.

Labeth wanted to object but kept silent. She couldn't stop thinking about the people, her people, huddled in their homes, watching as enemy soldiers walked their streets, scared for their lives, their property seized or damaged. While it had been ages since Loreiak had been at war, Labeth knew what enemies did to the places they conquered. How soon would it take for her people to lose hope that their crown would rescue them?

"What is the reading of the stars?" the queen asked the priest.

"Not favorable, Your Majesty."

Her mother's shoulder sunk even more. Special priests called star seers studied the movement of the stars in the sky and their relationship to each other and the planets to try to tell the future. It wasn't always accurate, Labeth reminded herself. But star readings were respected.

"Alright," said her mother. "No troops to retaliate. We'll focus on preserving the trade roads."

The meeting moved on to how to protect them and prepare the nearby cities and the capital for refugees. When the meeting was over and everyone dismissed, her mother asked Labeth to stay behind. "Why were you not here on time?" she demanded.

"I didn't sleep well last night, so I fell asleep again after my maidservant woke me. I'm sorry. It won't happened again."

"I'll have a servant bring you tea before you retire tonight. Make sure you get good sleep for a day of long meetings tomorrow. We'll have to start preparing for the refugees."

Labeth studied the map of Loreiak on the table, figurines placed over it to represent Loreiak's and Toa's troops. There were way more representing the Toa's ships than Loreiak's and they were closing in. The Toa flag stood where Resenmir was. "We're just going to let Resenmir go?"

"The stars are not shining favorably on us."

"They could be wrong."

"We have to think long-term." Her mother stared at the map as well, heaviness in the lines of her face. "It isn't the easy choice, but we can't attack the Toa right now. Not while we don't know what land weapons they have. It could be a slaughter, and we might not take back Resenmir anyway."

"There has to be something we can do," Labeth said softly. Leaving her people under the Toa's grasp made her want to scream in frustration. It wasn't right. It couldn't be right. "There has to be some solution—.",

"This is the solution." Her mother motioned to the room around them. "You have always been looking for a big fix, so you miss out what truly can help. I see you doze off during the citizen's supplications. You come late to your meetings. It's a disgrace!"

"It won't happen again, Mother."

"It better not," she said firmly. "Stop looking for fixes that aren't there and focus on what matters. The day-to-day work of coming up with battle strategies, hearing supplications, and making hard decisions. You win a war by winning battles and that is how you make a difference."

Labeth bowed her head, cowed and even more embarrassed at her late entry. She'd been doing well following her duties, but now the house of cards she'd crafted was tumbling down. She didn't like disappointing her mother, contrary to what the queen must think at times. She wanted to contribute, be useful. But how? What could she contribute to help Loreiak win this war?

They want our magic, Sorsetha had said. It was one thing the Toa didn't have that they wanted at all costs. "Have we thought of using mysticism to fight?" she offered.

"Mysticism has never lent itself well to fighting."

"Surely, there are ways we can use it to our advantage."

"Are you well practiced in the mystic arts?" her mother asked in a condescending tone. Why did she have to be that way, Labeth thought. She was trying. Her mother knew that she couldn't be skilled in the mystic arts, and Labeth wasn't going to mention the farseeking ritual she and Asanilph had done. "If you want to look further into using the mystic arts in warfare, you can. It is not a terrible suggestion, but demands more thought." She took Labeth by the arms. "It takes a lot to be a great queen. I push you because I want you to succeed. The crown is a great burden. Honor your people by carrying it."

"I know," Labeth replied.

Her mother squeezed her shoulders, which was more affection than she thought she would get but not as much as she wanted. "I won't be here always. Make sure when that day comes, you will be ready."

Labeth nodded and returned to her room, heavy with the burden of fear. Her mother was right. It'd been a disgrace to show up late as she had. Her people needed a responsible crown princess, not one who was careless enough to fall back asleep.

When Labeth reached her bedroom, Reshelia stood at her vanity, her back turned to her. Seeing her sister better immediately brightened her mood. "Resh, how are you feeling?"

"I'm fine," she said without conviction. She turned sideways enough for Labeth to see that she was fingering the cloak draped over her vanity's chair. It'd been the one she had worn last night, and dirt and fallen leaves stained its hem. She'd forgotten to put it with the dirty laundry. "You look tired."

Brushing it off, Labeth approached and rubbed Reshelia's small baby bump. "How's the baby?"

Reshelia pulled away. "Not kicking yet."

"It's still early," Labeth replied as Reshelia closed the doors between her bedroom and sitting room so they couldn't be overheard.

"You saw it again last night, didn't you?" whispered Reshelia. "You need to stop speaking with it."

No, not her too. Labeth had hoped that after Reshelia had experienced the beauty of the Jemalgee's song like she had that finally someone would understand their connection and that not all Jemalgee were evil. "He healed you. It's proof he's not like the others. Didn't you think his song was beautiful?"

"Beautiful?" asked Reshelia. "It was painful." Her voice cracked on the last word, and she finally faced Labeth, grief twisting her face. "All these thoughts—memories of him and that he's gone—thrown in my face. I couldn't hide from it."

Labeth took Reshelia's arms just like her mother had done to her. "You had to face your grief. It was killing you."

"I know." She broke into sobs, barely able to speak. "But it hurts so much—hurts so much. He's gone." She pressed her face into Labeth's shoulder. "I'm so alone."

"Resh," Labeth pulled back and held her sister's face. "I'm here. We're all here for you—mother, Asanilph, everyone in the palace. We'll help you raise the baby. You don't have to do this alone."

"I don't know if I can. . ." Her words faded into sobs.

"We can," she said. "I promise you we'll get through this." The words came out on instinct, and Labeth wondered how much truth they held. Here she was trying to encourage her sister when her own faith in their future was shaken by the war. She had feared that Reshelia would never rise from her catatonia, but they had found a way, and though Reshelia might never fully heal from losing Hithlin, it would get better. Grief was a natural part of life that everyone experienced and moved on from eventually.

The joy she had felt when Reshelia had finally awoken had restored her hope that they could still change things no matter how dark they seemed. She held onto that memory. She wasn't going to give up hope yet.

High Priest Dlanacen stared at Labeth with the uncomfortable gaze of a servant waiting for a command and who is unable to speak his mind. It was infuriating and made it impossible to focus on the heavy, leather-bound ritual book in her hands, so she ended up flipping through it distractedly and handed it to the servant standing behind her. "I'll take this one back to the palace with me," she said, returning to browse the shelves for more.

"Your Highness," said Dlanacen, "I can't allow that."

"Why?" she asked simply.

"These are our best books of the mystic arts. They cannot leave the Temple District's library."

"I am the Crown Princess, future ruler of the kingdom. I can take what I wish," Labeth replied, channeling her mother. Her words were a bit more condescending than they should've been, but Dlanacen irritated her so much. He always seemed to patronize her, though it might be that she was still holding a grudge from when he cast lightning into her to check that she hadn't been possessed by a Jemalgee. She grabbed another book from the shelf and handed it to the servant. "I'll take this one too."

She proceeded to pile on two more heavy books into the servant's arms before determining that she had enough to start her research. It'd been a couple of weeks since her mother had challenged her to find a way for them to use mysticism against the Toa. She'd started in the palace's library which hadn't contained anything useful and resolved that surely the Temple District's would have better offerings.

When she told Dlanacen that she was done, he led her out of the building while explaining in great detail how valuable the books that she was taking were, that she was to take care good care of them, never drink or eat near them, don't leave them out in the sun, and so on. On their way back to her carriage, they passed the Temple of Ghustaugness. Labeth glimpsed something through the doorway that made her pause.

"Can we go in there?" she asked, inclining her head.

"You won't find anything to help us win the war in there, I promise you that."

Masking her irritation, Labeth entered anyway. The temple was one big room and its walls were covered in drawings of sleep demons, tales of madness caused by dark magic, creatures of the Unfound World. Across from the door, a sculpture of a Jemalgee's true form leered over everything like the master sitting at the head of his table. A Jemalgee's true form was so massive the human eye could never perceive all of it—they were as big as mountains—so that was why they usually traveled as smoke. Though no one had seen one, it'd always been said that its true form was like a serpent with four legs and three sets of webbed wings. This sculpture had its wings flared out and its teeth bared, ready to attack.

So this is what he truly looked like, she thought. It was hard to reconcile the beauty of his song with the monstrous sculpture. The sculpture barred its teeth in such a wide, hungry grimace Labeth half-expected to see blood dripping from its mouth. It was unnerving.

As Dlanacen drew up beside her, she asked him, "Has there ever been an account of a Jemalgee returning to its place in the sky?"

"No. None could ever regain any bit of purity, much less what it would take to return to their first form."

"Why not? If darkness can come from light, cannot light come from darkness?"

"Not from the Ghustaugness. It devours all light before it has the chance to grow." He added in a low tone, "You need to put away this fascination with the Jemalgee. They are all evil, and you should stay as far away from them as possible."

For a moment, Labeth panicked that he knew she'd been in contact with one but put that fear away. He couldn't possibly know.

She surveyed the other drawings. "What about these? Are there any creatures we could control and use as weapons?" She was partially curious and partially hoping to draw attention away from the Jemalgee.

In one drawing, a creature with a skull and antlers of a deer twisted its torso at an ugly angle to hover over a dead man, his entrails scattered on the ground. Blood stained its snout, and its wholly black eye stared nowhere and everywhere at once. A dark mane flowed down its back, as black as its eyes, as black as the smoke of a Jemalgee. Beside it was another monster made from blood-stained bones. The drawings made Labeth's stomach turn. As they were intended to.

"Those are wendigos and gashads. Unless you want to destroy your own people along with the Toa, I suggest we do not try to use them," replied Dlanacen, his contempt for her idea obvious in his tone. He agreed with her mother—that her quest was a foolhardy one. "Wendigos not only devour human flesh but also infect people with their cannibalistic desires. And gashads are made from the bones of starving people. They lurk by trade roads and bite the heads of travelers and drink their blood." He motioned toward the rest of the monsters on the walls, saying, "All these creatures cannot be controlled, only avoided. They are solely capable of evil, having been born from the ultimate evil themselves."

"I want to cover all of our options," Labeth replied coldly. "But we can move on." He was right though she loathed to admit it.

She took all the books she'd selected back to her chambers and scanned them for anything useful. It didn't take long to prove her mother right—mysticism was not a type of magic that could be used as a powerful weapon. It was a magic of channels, mostly used for farseeking, to quicken healing, or to make forgetting or love potions and the like. The passages on mystic theory fascinated her the most, especially anything having to do about the ghustaugness. Lenou, the ultimate light, and ghustaugness, the ultimate darkness, existed on a spectrum in every creature with pure Jemalgee on the end and the corrupted ones on the other. Between them existed humans who possessed equal capacity for good and evil. Additionally, interacting with the darker side of mysticism corrupted a person, a fact known to everyone, but what wasn't talked about nearly as much was that this worked both ways. Light could drive out the darkness in humans as well.

Labeth continued to meet with the Jemalgee, though she had to space their rendezvous so she could catch up on sleep. He just wanted her to talk with him, and after the initial awkwardness faded, it became so easy to tell him everything. She told him things she'd never admitted to anyone else, and he didn't judge her, like a silent night absorbing every sound. With each visit, she saw more of his brokenness and his desire for redemption. And each night, she wished more to bring him any hope or peace she could offer. She'd leave him candles, though he said her presence was enough of a gift.

As she continued reading the mystic books and meeting with him, Labeth had an idea. A crazy idea but it wasn't her first—that had been asking the Jemalgee to save Reshelia and that had worked out. There was already goodness in him so if this plan was to work with any Jemalgee, it would be him.

That night was the sixth time she'd visited him. She passed under the tree's branches that looked like bird wings, rushing toward the cave. Though the climb was still long and difficult, she'd grown stronger and faster these past few weeks. She tried to get up and down the mountain as fast as she could now so she could squeeze some sleep in.

When she reached the cave, she went right in without calling out in greeting and placed her lantern on the cave floor and sat beside it. He came to her, tendrils of black smoke dancing around the lantern's flames like a moth and curling around her till she could no longer see the entrance. She wasn't scared though. The Jemalgee flowed over the stalactites and down to the boulders on the floor, the effect like the inside of a wave continually crashing.

"I have something to tell you," she said, her excitement permeating her voice.

"Your presence is enough," he replied.

"You're too kind," she said to act humble but the compliment made her beam. She loved that their meetings brought him peace, no matter how small. She loved meeting with him too. "I was reading through some mystic literature, and I think I know a way to redeem you."

The feel of the cave went cold as every puff of black smoke stilled. Labeth blushed, sobered. That had not been the reaction she'd been expecting. Was something wrong?

"Impossible," he said.

"It's not. We can do thi—."

"I told you there was no way!"

"Just hear me out!" She'd dreamed how this conversation would go, but it was falling quickly out of that picture. "Mysticism is a magic of channels with humans acting as the ultimate channel. Light and darkness flow in and out of us, and we are the main controllers of channeling magic. If you were to take a human host, I believe that over time their soul could help grow the goodness in you and purify your soul."

"There's nothing left to grow." His voice echoed in the cave.

"But I've seen it. Several times." She raised her voice to compete with his. "You saved me and my sister," she said, unintentionally repeating what she had written in her poem for him. "You couldn't bring her from the darkness if there wasn't light in you to guide her. And you wish to do good. Isn't that enough? I don't care what legend says. I know what I see. They're all wrong. Don't give up hope."

"When I take a host, my soul floods in, washing away theirs into a pit where they may watch, scream, and beg, but never act. I burn through their goodness till it dies under darkness' demand. All will fall under its weight. None are special and no hope is eternal to save me."

"I don't mean possession. What I'm suggesting is something deeper. More complete. A full joining of souls so that they are one and cannot be separated. It would require a ritual, which I am still trying to find. But I'm close." I just wanted to tell you already, she thought. She had hoped that once she'd told him that redemption was possible, he would be happy and thankful, but his negative reaction made her feel foolish. The shadows of her doubts crept closer. Maybe she was foolish like everyone seemed to think.

"Have you found the host?"

"I don't know," she mumbled. She'd thought of a candidate, but the idea had seemed crazier than anything she'd dreamed up thus far. She wasn't ready to decide.

Footsteps crunched on the cave floor behind them. Scared she'd been followed, Labeth turned as a woman walked into the circle of light. She was blonde and of similar age to her but sauntered with arrogance. Her clothes were that of a peasant, and her long, straight hair hung free around her.

"So this is what you've left me for," she said, eying Labeth with distaste. There was a lilt to her voice that was familiar but unique in its abnormality.

"You're not welcome here," the Jemalgee replied, his voice low like a beast's growl.

"I don't care. Who are you?" The last part was directed at Labeth.

"I'm a servant girl from the palace," she made up on the spot. Instinct told her to not reveal who she really was.

The other girl's lips drew back, baring her teeth in an animalistic grin. Her canines seemed too sharp, her grin too wide.

"Don't disrespect me by lying, Crown Princess. I know who you are, but what am I?" she sang like a child playing a game.

Something touched Labeth's soul like a hand brushing her cheek. She sprang to her feet and jerked back but could not escape the touch, and gooseflesh spread over her body as the revelation hit her. It was another Jemalgee. Her voice's lilt was the same as the other's, but her soul's touch stung like a viper.

"What are you doing out here?" it continued. "Shouldn't you be trying to convince more soldiers to die for you?"

Labeth flinched. Like all Jemalgee, this one could read her like a book and knew where to hit. For the first time, Labeth knew how awful soul reading felt when coming from a place of cruelty rather than healing. No wonder there were so many horrible accounts of this power.

"Stop it," ordered the Jemalgee she knew. "Labeth, go."

The new Jemalgee's touch fell away, and Labeth grabbed her lantern and left. She didn't slow down till she passed the tree with branches like bird wings, her old fear of the Jemalgee having been reignited at meeting this new one. But it didn't shake her faith that her Jemalgee was different than the rest of his kind.

When she returned to the palace, for the next couple of weeks, she threw herself into studying mysticism. There was no ritual to do what she wanted, but that didn't mean she couldn't make one. When she had something she thought would work, she returned to his cave. But he wasn't there.

Dior

That was one of the worst nights of my life. I stayed outside that cave the whole time you two conspired to take you away from me forever. I didn't realize she would be there but had meant to surprise you with the host I had taken. I wanted to strangle her. Slowly. We would have both been better off with her dead.

I thought my plan was better. Take a form like that girl's so you could fuck her. You've always had a thing for the ones pure of heart. And blondes. You love exposing them to the darkest of pleasures no matter how much you deny it. I could've gotten her for you, but of course you wouldn't have allowed that. That way we could get this obsession of yours out and move on. You should've stayed with me.

Our history is written in the absence of stars, you and I. We used to shine as the eyes of the Circling Fish as the first humans called it. I revolved around you. When you shone, I glistened. And when you came to their world, took one of their bodies to drink in their physical sensation, I watched. And when you could not return, when you were consumed by the ghustaugness, I joined you.

For thousands of years, we feasted. Though you were the first, you were never fully like the others of our kind that followed us from the sky. They rejoiced in their freedom, but you, you liked to mourn. I could make you forget (for a time). But you never got over it. And look at where your self-pity has gotten you.

I tried my best to stop you from making this mistake. You should've thanked me for that. Though she didn't tell you, I read from her soul the intentions of using herself as the host to purify you. The arrogance of that little bitch! I did what I did next for all of us. For you to lose interest in her, for the ritual to not work for lack of a "pure" vessel, and for her to be brought low like the rest of us. Let her eat the dust. It was good for her.

(I couldn't let you leave me).

V

Saying the ritual's words, Labeth sent her mind out to look for the Jemalgee. She circled like a hawk over Mt. Raseynor, dove between its trees, over the lake, before continuing down into the streets of Soros Cereminir. He was nowhere to be found. She couldn't go farther without anyone to help her extend her reach, so she made sure her search was thorough.

Her vision dissolved, and she smelled ash. It was so strong she felt it in her lungs and coughed it out, her concentration breaking and ending the ritual. Her throat was dry and the coughs shook her deeply. When the fit was over, she leaned back against the rock. She was at her favorite writing spot. She'd come here several times in the past couple of weeks, hoping that the Jemalgee would meet her, but he never did. Eventually, she'd gotten tired of waiting and tried the farseeking ritual, but she must have done something wrong. She didn't know what had just happened or if it was a common way for rituals to go awry.

Tilting her head back, she stared up at the moon. It was high in the sky and beautiful. It was time for her to return to the palace if she was to get any sleep so her mother wouldn't grow suspicious.

As Labeth blew out the candle and packed up her things, a beautiful voice soared on the wind, coming from below. At first, it sounded like a Jemalgee's but it wasn't quite perfect and otherworldly enough. Labeth peered over the edge of the cliff and found a woman bathing in the lake and singing. She was naked and stood so from hip up she was exposed. Labeth flushed and warmed with desire. She wanted to keep watching but propriety made her look away.

She retreated toward the woods, scared to make a sound or stand where she could be seen. That woman had been beautiful with honeyed-brown hair and round breasts. Ashamed, Labeth pushed the images from her mind, but the woman's voice followed her down the mountain. No matter how much she tried to ignore it, it wove its way into her heart and ran circles around her mind till she knew the melody by heart—till she hummed it herself long after she couldn't hear it anymore. Even when she fell asleep, it played in her dreams.

She went back three days later when usually she waited a full week before sneaking out. She told herself it wasn't to see if the woman would be there again as her feet led her up the familiar path to her writing spot. But when she reached the fork in the road, she heard the song again and turned onto the path to the lake.

What was she doing, she thought. This was obscene. She was no peeping tom.

When she managed to get herself to stop walking, it was too late; she could see her through the trees. Rising from the water, she put on a thick robe and began combing her hair. "Are you going to say hello?" she said in a sing-song voice.

It took a moment for Labeth to realize that she was talking to her. With a panicked squeak, Labeth ducked behind a tree.

"Aw, come on. Don't be shy," the woman said. "Let me see you. I know you've seen me."

Face blazing hot, Labeth shuffled from behind the tree and into the clearing. "I'm so sorry," she stammered, looking any-where but at the woman.

The woman chuckled. "It's fine," she said and leaned against a tree. "What's your name?"

Labeth sneaked a glance at her face. The way she looked at her made Labeth's stomach flip, for the glimmer in her eyes made it seem like Labeth was the most intriguing, wonderful thing. Like in the peaceful night under a full moon with many stars, by a shining lake, and while serenaded by crickets and the rustle of leaves, Labeth was still the most beautiful thing to focus on.

"Josa," she replied, thinking it wasn't a good idea to reveal she was the crown princess to a stranger. She also didn't want that part of her identity lurking over her tonight. She didn't want her life. She wanted now.

"Beautiful name," the woman replied like she was compli-menting more than just the name. Blushing deeper, Labeth stam-mered thanks. "Come eat with me." The woman motioned to a blanket that had been laid by the edge of the lake, a wicker basket sitting on it. Without waiting for a reply, she took Labeth's hand and led her to sit. When she let go, Labeth's hand still tingled.

From the basket, the woman drew out bread, cheese, some apples, and a knife. She cut everything up and laid it out on the blanket. "Go on. Eat," she said with a smile and motioned to the food with the knife. The moon's bright blue light reflected off its sharp edge. Labeth obeyed. The cheese was buttery and the bread crisp and soft where it needed to be. And the apple's juice was so sweet and fresh it must have been grown recently, though it was in the middle of winter.

"You must be so cold," said Labeth.

The woman looked at her quizzically.

"The water. It must be freezing this time of year. How do you bathe in it?" added Labeth, trying to not seem so awkward.

"I like the cold. It wakes me up." She leaned back on one arm, and the collar of her robe opened enough to show a strip of gooseflesh running up her chest. "And what are you doing out here?"

"I like to write. Up there." Labeth motioned to the cliff atop the waterfall. "But when I heard you sing, I couldn't help but to follow it."

The woman laughed. "I was hoping you would notice it," she said, taking a bite of an apple.

"You knew I was up there?"

"I could see the light of your candle and I was curious what was up there. Glad it was you," she added with a smile that made Labeth's toes curl with self-consciousness. Why was this woman treating her so? She didn't really think she was that. . .beautiful? Interesting?

"You didn't tell me your name," Labeth replied to steer the conversation away from herself.

"Phieydior." Her voice glided through the vowels like waves crashing, ending with the roll of the 'r'. Labeth wished for her to say it again.

"I've never heard that name before."

"It's an old one, but you may call me Dior for short."

As they continued eating, Dior asked about Labeth, what she liked to write, why the cliff was her favorite writing spot, and Labeth found herself growing more comfortable with the other woman, their bodies shifting closer to each other's.

"What else do you do out here besides write?" Dior asked.

Labeth stopped herself from taking another bite of her apple. "What do you mean?"

"Come now. I know there's something you're not telling me." Smiling, Dior pushed Labeth's shoulder with hers. "I want to know you. Tell me everything."

Blushing, Labeth took another bite to give herself time to think. No one understood her connection with the Jemalgee, not even her sister whom he had saved, so Dior couldn't be different. But the way Dior looked and talked to her, like she already cherished Labeth for who she was, made her hope differently.

"I'm trying to reach a Jemalgee," she confessed.

Dior's eyes widened, but she didn't pull away. "Why?"

"He's not like the others of his kind. He's helped me before, and I want to return the favor. I think I know a way that he can be redeemed and return to the sky."

"How?"

Labeth told her about what she had discovered of the fundamentals of mysticism and the ritual she had made since the last time she'd spoken with the Jemalgee. "It requires a host strong enough to share their goodness with him and purify him. And I was planning on offering myself as it," Labeth added what she hadn't dared to tell the Jemalgee.

"That's very selfless of you," said Dior, thankfully not judging her like everyone else.

"He ran off when I told him, and I haven't been able to find him since."

Dior smoothed a lock of hair away from Labeth's face, drawing her out of her stupor. "You'll find him. He might be closer than you think. But while we wait, why not entertain ourselves?" And she kissed her.

Labeth found herself kissing back. She didn't have a lot of experience with sex—it wasn't easy to determine who was her type and she'd never been brazen in going after what she wanted like others. So when Dior began loosening the ties of her clothes, she pulled away, too nervous and overwhelmed to continue. She liked kissing Dior, but she wasn't ready to go further.

"I'm sorry," she began to stammer. "This was nice, but I should get back."

"Stay," Dior breathed. While she leaned in for another kiss, she reached up Labeth's skirt.

Labeth flinched away, shocked at Dior's forwardness. "No, maybe another night."

Dior's eyes lit up and her lips pulled into a cruel smile. "Have to admit I was hoping for things to go this way," she said, her voice rhythmic like a song. She slapped her.

Labeth fell against the blanket, dazed, and Dior knelt on her stomach so she couldn't regain her breath. The blade of the knife pressed cold into the underside of her jaw as Dior's face leered so closely over hers like she intended to kiss her again. Labeth's left cheek burned, and she realized the other woman hadn't slapped her but had hit her with the knife.

"Let go of me!" Labeth gasped, unable to gather enough breath to speak louder.

"Is this not what you wanted?" Dior asked mockingly. "Why you return to your perch to call and call my name, my bird? You desire to be one?" As one hand pulled at Labeth's undergarments, another—incorporeal—slithered under her skin, and she felt the chilling touch of a Jemalgee. "It's me. Your Jemalgee."

Labeth yelped in pain as Dior pushed further. "No, you're not him."

"Of course, it's me. This is who I am."

"No. You're that other one," Labeth spit out. "He would never do this to me."

Dior sighed, some of the glee leaving her. "Fine," she said, dragging out the word. "I had hoped for that game to last a little longer, but instead let us get to the best of parts."

Labeth cried out as a burning pain scraped between her legs. She grabbed the food basket and swung it into Dior's head so hard it forced the Jemalgee off of her. Labeth got to her feet and ran, grabbing the knife Dior had dropped. It didn't take long for the Jemalgee to catch up and tackle her. They wrestled on the ground in a tangle of arms and legs using every muscle to gain leverage. Labeth couldn't see anything but arms, robe, hair, and that terrible smile of Dior. There was no doubt that the Jemalgee wanted—desired—to hurt her.

Labeth still held the knife. She saw a flash of skin and stabbed.

They broke apart, and heaving, Labeth propped herself up into a sitting position against a tree. Dior lay on the ground, examining her thigh, the knife sticking out of it. She pulled it out without hesitation and grinned at Labeth. "Not a great feeling for me, but you did much more damage to my vessel. She'll always walk with a limp after this, 'less you kill her."

Labeth tried to run again, but Dior grabbed her shoulders and knocked her head into the tree so hard she collapsed, unable to move till the blackness cleared.

And Dior pinned her to the ground and had her way with her. She stripped her naked, marred her body with tiny cuts, and did things that Labeth would never be able to forget. The pain and helplessness were excruciating. And the worst part were the words Dior sang—a Jemalgee's poem dedicated to her:

> "Labeth, my bird, no matter the stories she's heard
> seeks to save darkness from itself with herself
> because she is so pure, Labeth, my bird.
> So gracious and generous,
> loving and naive.

So full of hubris, she's foolish
enough to carry our disease.

Labeth, my bird, or 'cause of the stories she's heard
wants no matter the cost to matter lest she's
the princess, the daughter who's left out of favor?
	Too silly and uncanny
	to lead a nation at peace.
	She'll fail the future.
	Obvious enough—everyone sees.

Labeth, my bird, why are you weeping?
You asked to reap this darkness,
and you'll burn by the tortures you've heard."

The song scratched at her every insecurity, and just as she couldn't fight against Dior's hands, she couldn't fight against them. Everyone else had been right when they had told her to stay away from the Jemalgee. She was a humiliation. An idiot. A part of her wished Dior intended to kill her because she didn't know how she could go on living after this.

But Dior didn't kill her. Once done, she spit on her and said, "Try taking him away from me now, whore." Standing, she plunged the knife into the body of her host. A tunnel of black smoke flew out of the woman's mouth, and she crumpled, landing beside Labeth, no longer possessed. Dior abandoned them to die.

As the woman coughed blood and looked at her for help, Labeth remained where she lay in shock. There was nothing she could do since she couldn't even help herself, so she watched the other woman die as the moon began its descent and the night grew darker.

Jemalgee

I HID MYSELF IN THE OPPOSITE CORNER of Loreiak to stay away from you. I was so scared of hurting you that I did not think of what Dior would do. She's petty but usually harmless.

I hid in the most remote part of the Laluv Forest, but as always, Dior found me. It is easier to avoid humanity than it is her, because she searches ceaselessly and can travel quickly to find where I am. That's why I didn't run. There was no point. And I'm glad I stayed, otherwise I wouldn't have found out what she'd done to you. It made tolerating her company for a few minutes worth it.

She bragged about raping you, singing the words out in a jaunty tune. I threw her against the tree, but she dispersed, unharmed. If only I could truly hurt her. . . . I would give anything. I would rip her body apart with teeth if I had them. I roared at her like I had never done before because this time, though I am a master of language, a creature who can turn other's deepest feelings into poetry, I couldn't find the words to express the anger and anguish I felt.

I hope I have not ever been so horrendous as Dior but I know I have. But I would never hurt you, so maybe you are right. I am different from the rest of my kind.

I lunged at Dior, and we twisted through the air to strike like vipers. We could have wrestled all night, all eternity, but still not have been able to hurt one another. Only lightning can do that, and that element was forever lost to us a long time ago.

She raved against you, saying I should be thankful, but the second she let slip that she had left you alive, I ran to you. I was back at Mt. Raseynor in minutes and scoured the mountainside with my senses for you. When I found you, you fell backward, screaming. I'll never forget your horror when you didn't recognize me. Please, don't look at me like that again.

But once you saw it was me, you calmed. You wore only a robe, its front covered in the red-purplish stain of dried blood. A cut scarred your cheek, and you looked bruised and battered, your hair a mess. I was so furious at Dior I could have torn down mountains, but I had to get you to safety.

When I took you in my arms, you were so small, insignificant to a creature of my greatness and power. But I would do anything to keep you safe.

When we reached the palace, I stopped at its boundary; the priests had coated the dirt with a thick line of obsidian rock that circled the grounds. I laid you down and roared to get the guards' attention. All over, they abandoned their posts to run toward me, but it took almost half a minute for the first one to arrive, so slow compared to how fast I can move. If not for the boundary, I could've killed them all already, and I had to remind myself that I was not there to destroy anyone.

When the first guard arrived, he recognized you and lunged forward but stopped when he saw me. I drew back some but stayed close. That coward wouldn't face me to save you, his princess. I wanted to twist his head around like opening a bottle.

He finally did his duty when I threatened him to take you. As he took you to the palace, other guards arrived. One lit the tip of his arrow on fire and shot it at me. I dodged easily but remained as docile as I could stand. Where was the queen? Time means nothing to me, but waiting there tested my restraint.

Eventually, she came with several priests; the one closest to her had an obvious air of self-importance that I didn't need my extra senses to know. They stayed on the other side of the boundary, smart to be wary of me.

"What do you want?" your mother demanded. Everyone thought I'd been the one to do this to you, and it was sad that even the most powerful woman of this country still sought to appease me rather than attack.

I explained what happened but they didn't trust me, barely even listened, unlike you. You are so strange. The only way I could make them understand was if I sang my own soul to them. I imbued the words with my deepest emotions, so they couldn't deny my truth nor my love for you. I also shared the memory of Dior telling me what she had done.

It worked. They listened, something I did not think possible. But I think I can owe it partially to your mother. She is not inclined to mercy like you. She wanted revenge. And I was glad to give it to her.

Your daughter has shown me kindness, a drop
of water in the desert I have traveled
through since before this continent was formed.
And like a thirsty man, I never would
destroy what gave me life—intentionally.
I fled in order to protect her from
my nature, but another did this as
revenge against me. Let me make this right
and drag that petty piece of shit under
your blade so she will know a thousand cuts
for every one she carved on your daughter.

Dior

When you fled from the Laluv Forest, I thought truly (for the first time) that that was the end of us. You didn't waste the breath to scream at me when you found out I'd left her alive. (Am I that meaningless to you?) The woods were dark, but as not as dark as us. Though the canopy obscured most of the sky, I could still feel our kind humming from their constellations, and even the barest wisp of their light made me sick. They didn't want you! They didn't love you! (Not like me).

—Who followed you into the unknown? Who has stood by your side while the ones above watched you suffer—I yelled into the night though you were too far to hear me.

I went into the nearest city, possessed the butcher, and made him carve meat of his family. Such was my fury that only the tension of human muscle as it stabbed, struck, and slaughtered could express it. You would've been horrified to see it. Perhaps you shouldn't have left me. That would've stopped it.

A few days later, I took another host inside Soros Cereminir so you would know where to find me when/if you returned to me. I still hadn't lost hope for us. And you did come back. You wore the host of a prostitute (that's how I knew you were really returning to me) whose body was dressed in jewels, a flowy skirt, and a see-through lace top that covered her waist and gathered with fabric over her breasts. Her black curls were pinned from her face, showing off your dark, demure smile.

I pulled you into my arms. I was wearing the host of a shop-keeper in her mid-thirties with brittle, brown hair. I'd taken her because she was close by, and I didn't want to draw attention to myself with a more attractive host. When we kissed, it was like tasting purpose again. This—such a lovely thing as us—was what I was meant for. What we were meant for.

"You see now?" I asked you.

You nodded. "I'll never suffer for fools again when I've you in my arms and all pleasure is ours."

I didn't search your soul to see if you were lying for I trusted you (even then). When I kissed you again, running my hand up your thigh, you pulled away and said you knew somewhere secluded. We kept our fingers interlaced (I was so loathed to release you) as you led me through the marketplace. I remember admiring your hair and the beautiful pin keeping it in place. It was shaped like a wasp, its body made of amber. The creature's beauty and danger fit you.

We entered into the back room of a whore house where there was a large deep sofa and a table filled with gold and jewels.

"I brought these for you." You picked up a gold necklace and wound its chain around your fingers.

Taking your hand, I kissed your gold chain covered knuckles and pulled you close so I could whisper in your ear, "I'd like to see you wear them. And only them."

As you changed to oblige me, I couldn't stop my curiosity for joy had loosened my lips. "She turned you away, didn't she? Beautiful Labeth, not full of grace after all. I knew her round, blue eyes were only full of compassion because she hadn't comprehended who you really are. So I fixed that issue."

Once you were finished, you turned around and sat on the table. "Befriending her was a mistake." True regret shown shiny on your face—something I wouldn't truly comprehend till later. You spread your legs and said, "Show me what I can never get from her."

The time for grief was over. I kissed your mouth, your neck, your breasts, so delighted to be back, flesh against flesh. The two of us. Forever. You dangled my desire for you on a spit, so you could strike when it would hurt the most.

Pain flashed through my left shoulder, and I fell back onto the floor, hissing in pain. I pulled the hairpin from my shoulder and dropped it onto the rug, my hand weak and shaky. All my senses dimmed, and I felt so, so tired. You'd drugged me. Instinctively, I made to dispossess my host, but I couldn't.

You yelled something, but a haze had come over me, making it hard to focus. I heard two thuds, and one of the tapestries lifted, pushed open by a hidden door. Men dressed in robes entered. I didn't know yet that they were Loreiakian priests or that it was their doing I was trapped in my host, for I would never give creatures so beneath my station any sort of care.

Mumbling something, they bound my arms and legs, and I could not fight. I hadn't known what it meant to be scared before then, and I have you to thank for that. I am a Jemalgee. To be scared is the anti-thesis of all the greatness of our kind, and you debased even that. As if spitting on my love wasn't enough for you. I should've listened to everyone. You are nothing but a traitor.

You knelt by my feet, smiling that dark, demure smile. "You have much to pay for."

"Make them stop," I pleaded, cause in those days I still wished for you to turn back and save me. "Or kill me now." If my vessel died, at least I'd be free. "That will be painful enough," I added, hoping that would satisfy your vengeance.

"I am not the one who deserves to make you suffer," you replied.

I went rigid. Even when you came to exact your revenge, it was only for her to do. Everything was only ever for her.

VI

LABETH WAS NUMB. The elixir they'd given her for the pain and the nightmares made her sluggish and unable to feel even the soft down of her bed. She lay on her stomach, her head just off the pillow and face half-buried, so she breathed into the mattress. She looked at herself in her mirror's vanity, as if it could tell her what she was feeling and who she was, for the images of mirrors and glass were the duals of thoughts. But she saw nothing in herself.

A soft knock sounded at her open bedroom door followed by footsteps. Labeth didn't stir but let Sorsetha pull her into a sitting position against her headboard and place a tray of food in her lap. The mystic healer pushed Labeth's hair out of her face with her wrinkled hands, stroking it all the way to its ends like a mother does for her child.

"I brought crumpets with ham and eggs, your favorite," she said, but Labeth didn't acknowledge her. A few months ago it had been Reshelia locked in her grief and Labeth pleading for a response on the outside. Now Labeth was in her place as if Fate demanded it as the price for saving her sister.

"Let me cut the ham for you," said Sorsetha, breezing by the silence, trying to act like everything was okay when it was not. When she picked up the knife, the sun coming through the bedroom windows glinted off of its blade. Dior breathed in Labeth's face as she sang, her breath hot and smile wide. Labeth cried out and heard the sound of the knife piercing flesh.

A shattering of glass. Pounding of hands against the immovable body of another that trapped her, invaded her. And screams.

Labeth screamed and thrashed in her bed, pushing the food tray and blankets off. She couldn't stop. Her heart beat so fast and felt so large in her chest she thought she would stop breathing, yet she always had breath enough to scream. Hands gently grabbed her arms, but in her panic their soft hold was like the vice grip of Dior. They sat on her legs too. Dior was back. She wasn't finished.

Labeth screamed anew, but it devolved into sobs. When she felt herself losing strength, she gave up to the torment. She couldn't escape. No new torment came, but none of the old left. Once she stopped struggling, the body released her, and she curled onto her side into her soft mattress—cold like the ground—and cried till she slept.

No knife appeared with the next meal. No utensils at all. Just a sandwich of ham and cheese, something she could eat with her fingers or be fed if necessary. Sorsetha helped feed her, bathe her, dress her, and treated her wounds along with any other house-keeping chores that would allow her to stay near to keep an eye on Labeth. A guard always stood in her chamber's sitting room. Other than those two people, Labeth had hardly seen anyone for days. There were periods where Sorsetha would be gone but a guard always remained. It depressed her to be without true company and without true privacy.

One time while Sorsetha was gone, Labeth rose from bed. Her legs had been getting restless as her body slowly healed. Many of the bruises were fading, but the cuts still had a long way to heal and they would scar. She hated looking at them and hated herself more for it—hated that she was so vain as to grieve the loss of her smooth skin. She walked gingerly over to her desk, an ache re-awakening in her genitals with each step, and eased into the chair.

"Your Highness, do you need anything?" the guard called from the other room.

"No, I'm fine," Labeth replied without thinking, wanting him to leave her alone. She pressed a hand to her mouth to suppress the sob that ripped out of her. She was most definitely not fine.

Her desk was a mess as usual but there was a conspicuous dent of nothing in the middle. The priests had confiscated all of her research on mysticism and the Jemalgee.

When her Jemalgee had returned her to the palace, a guard had taken her to her rooms where Sorsetha had been waiting to treat her wounds. She'd given her a potion for the pain and stitched up her cuts. It'd been a couple of hours before Labeth's mother came to see her.

She'd been furious.

"What have you done?"

"I thought you had learned not to sneak out of the palace!"

"These creatures are evil. You should've known that. What were you thinking?"

When her mother had seen the books and papers on her desk with the damning evidence of Labeth's fascination with the Jemalgee, she had ordered Dlanacen in a cold voice to take them away. With a disdainful glance at Labeth, he had done so. Labeth said nothing through it all. She had known it was dangerous, that others would think her foolish. But she thought she had caught onto something beautiful no one else had. That she could save a Jemalgee and thus prove that no evil could not be overcome by the goodness of those who believed and tried.

How idiotic it all seemed now. She'd played with the ghustaugness and gotten burned. This was all her fault.

Labeth, my bird. So gracious and generous, loving and naive. So full of hubris, she's foolish enough to carry our disease. Dior's words came to back to her. She'd never forget them.

She grabbed one of her journals and flipped to a random page with a poem she'd written. The words were full of idiocy and naivete. She ripped out the page, crumpled it, and threw it to the side. And she kept ripping page after page out of the book. When she tired of that journal, she did the same to others she'd kept over the years and any loose papers, anything that held her words she'd been so arrogant to believe could matter. As she destroyed her work, she cried out in pain like she was destroying herself. She threw the disemboweled books against her balcony doors, making the wood and glass rattle like in a thunderstorm.

Hands clasped her wrists. No, not again.

"Labeth! Stop it!" A hand stroked her cheek, pulling her out of her sorrow enough to see that it was Reshelia who touched her. Mumbling soothing words, her sister removed the books from her hands and pulled her down to sit beside her on the floor. Labeth lay her head on Reshelia's lap, against her pregnant belly, and her sister stroked her hair and face.

When Labeth had calmed, Reshelia asked why she had turned on her books.

"All the poems are stupid. I hate them," said Labeth, her voice full of tears. "They're the drivel of an idiot."

"You're not an idiot."

"It's all my fault! I got myself into this mess, even after everyone said to stay away. I'm so stupid." She repeated, as if she could hurt herself with her words. Repetition was after all a poetic device, and these ravings against herself would be the only poetry she could write anymore.

Reshelia pushed Labeth into a sitting position and took her by the shoulders. "It wasn't your fault. It is never your fault." She said each word with great conviction, and her eyes glimmered with tears.

"But I knew how dangerous the Jemalgee are, and I still went out of the palace."

"You didn't know it would happen," Reshelia said. "Was this the same Jemalgee I met?"

"No, he would never hurt me," Labeth responded quickly. "He was the one that carried me back to the palace. It was another one. She seemed to not like that I was talking to him, and that's why. . ." As a new series of sobs started, Labeth covered her face with her hand. "I shouldn't have gotten involved. It was all so stupid." There was that word again. No matter how many times she repeated it, it didn't seem enough.

"It wasn't all bad. You got him to heal me. If it weren't for you," Reshelia took one of Labeth's hands from her face and put it on her belly, "she'd be dead."

"She?"

"It has to be a girl, right? Just has too," Reshelia said with a smile and a lightheartedness that had been missing from Labeth's life for so long.

They fell silent, staying like that—Labeth's hand on her sister's belly. After a minute, Labeth felt movement—a flash of pressure from inside her sister's stomach, a kick. For the first time in days, Labeth smiled.

"See," said her sister. "She wouldn't be here without you. I wouldn't be here. You did good."

It was true. But so was what had happened to her. Would she have caught the ire of Dior if she hadn't saved her sister? Probably not. Would she go back to leave her sister to waste away knowing what she did now? No. Evil had met her down this path. But so had some good.

"How are you able to go on?" She didn't have to say Hithlin's name for Reshelia to understand.

A weight came over her sister's face. "You," she said, her voice strained. "Her," she said, motioning to the baby with her chin. "Mother. Asanilph. The sweet cakes that the kitchen makes every Saturday evening with cinnamon on top." They both laughed despite their sorrow. "And the spring. I'm waiting for it. To see everything bloom again and feel its warmth. I have a list of what I enjoy and have to look forward to, no matter how small, and I remind myself that Hithlin would want me to enjoy them. Everyone tells me that one day it will get better. And it has. But it's still hard. And I still keep hoping. You showed me that." She took Labeth's hand and rubbed it with her thumb. "How to never give up hope."

Labeth was speechless. She would've never guessed that she had such an effect on her sister. She had struggled to hold on to her hope as well; it was the throughline that weaved through her fascination with the Jemalgee. It warmed her to know that she had a positive effect on anyone, and not just because she'd convinced the Jemalgee to heal her sister, but because of who she was.

"Thank you," was all she said. Was all she could say. Inadequate, but she wouldn't worry about that now.

A woman dangled from chains in the middle of the Temple of Blood. She was naked and limp, held so high by the chains that only the tips of her feet touched the black stone. Everything in the Temple of Blood was as black as night, black floor, black pillars, black altar. Only slivers of gold wound through all the stone like tributaries, and the torches glinting off of them gave the temple a hellish gleam. Labeth hated this temple and only entered for her monthly blood sacrifices. Blood was Life. Blood was good fortune on the land, for its people, so all made sacrifices for the good times to continue. Labeth obeyed the tradition, but the stink and sight of blood nauseated her. She didn't like to think of all the good of her country coming from such a disgusting practice, though she didn't deny its truth.

Whenever Labeth came, there was always a large animal, usually a pig or a deer, dangling from the chains as its blood drained into the depressed circle in the floor beneath. Never had there been a human. Human sacrifices had fallen out of favor in the last century, reserved only to appease Jemalgee or in the most dire of circumstances.

It was the middle of the night. Her mother had woken her and told her to get dressed but hadn't elaborated on where they were going. It'd been the first time they had seen each other in a week, since it'd happened. The carriage ride over had been long and eerily silent. Her mother hadn't said a word, and the streets were mostly empty as the majority of the city was asleep. Labeth never got to see Soros Cereminir like this. Whenever she'd been able to sneak off, it had been early enough in the evening to enjoy the nightlife, and her mother definitely would never allow her to go out so late. There was never a reason for a member of the royal family to do so. She had no idea what this was about.

The naked woman before her, already with a bloody shoulder, was something she never could have expected in a million years.

In the temple with them were Dlanacen on one side of the woman and the Jemalgee on the other. Labeth almost didn't believe her eyes at first when she saw him, his black smoke flowing up the wall like a reverse waterfall. The Jemalgee, here? With the High Priest and her mother? Was she dreaming? What madness was this?

"What is this?" she demanded of her mother. "Why am I here?"

"With the help of this Jemalgee," her mother nodded in respect toward him, "we have apprehended the one who hurt you."

When Labeth looked again at the woman, she recognized the cruel delight in Dior's smile and eyes, partially hidden beneath the hair of her host. They were too close. She was upon her, laughing in her face as her hands violated her. She couldn't run. She couldn't run.

Trembling, Labeth backed away, but her mother stopped her. "It cannot hurt you. We've bound it to this body temporarily, so it cannot leave its vessel."

"Take me back to the palace!" Labeth hissed, breathless. She needed to get away.

"You have to face this." Her mother's grip tightened on her arms. "It must be judged for what it's done, and I'll not have my daughter live in this agony. Face it, and you will be free."

Labeth was so confused. What did she mean? What could she do to make this pain go away? To be able to sleep through the night? To not see Dior's cruelty flash across her mind's eye every moment?

The queen led her forward, and when they approached the depressed circle, Dlanacen bowed low and held out a whip. Labeth would've liked to say that she didn't understand—that those kinds of thoughts would never occur to her—but she did. Other than a wound on her shoulder, there was not a mark on the naked body of Dior's host. Not yet.

"I can't," she stammered, trying to retreat but her mother held firm.

"Yes, you can," said her mother.

"But what about her vessel?" she asked, stalling. "She doesn't look like a prisoner. She doesn't deserve this."

"You are right," confirmed Dlanacen. "But I'm afraid we cannot force her to choose another vessel. It will have to be this way."

She felt like throwing up. At some point, the whip made its way into her hand and she was in the pit with Dior, alone, her mother finally backing off. Though the stone was black to hide as many blood stains as possible, there was still a faint discoloration in the pit. No matter how often the acolytes scrubbed the floor, they could never clean it all away.

Dior's host was a woman in her thirties, handsome in a plain way, but when the Jemalgee inside sneered, her face twisted into something ugly, eyes wide with madness and a smile full of hate. Blood coated her front teeth where someone had taken the liberty of first strike.

"Go on," she whispered like they were secret lovers trying to stay quiet. "I know you want to."

Did Dior just read her soul? No, Labeth would've felt it. How did she know though about the times late at night when Labeth had imagined driving the knife, not through her previous host's thigh, but through her heart? How her body ached with regret at the missed opportunity? She wished she'd done it. So badly. And she hated herself for considering killing an innocent in the process. For considering hurting another again.

She looked at her Jemalgee, all this time silent against the wall. Is this what he felt? Was this the ghustaugness pulling her down into its pit where she would get lost in the darkness of her nature? She already didn't recognize herself. It was there in the books: that humans had equal capacity for good and evil. But she had been so arrogant to think that she was too good for evil to have a foothold inside her heart; so good that she could house the worst of beings and purify it.

But she wanted revenge like the rest of them. And she didn't know how to be any different.

"Even if you do whip me, I've no regrets. I enjoyed every second of it." Dior half-moaned the words. "As I'm sure you did too."

That shocked Labeth out of her thoughts. "It was the worst thing I've ever been through in my life!"

"You wanted the taste of a Jemalgee." She licked her bloody, bottom lip.

"Stop it!" yelled Labeth, lost in rage and panic. She tried to remember Reshelia's words. *It wasn't your fault. It is never your fault.* But Dior's words rang truer to what she believed. That she'd been a fool and to blame for what had happened.

"You didn't heed the danger, because it entices you."

She screamed at her, and later she wouldn't be able to recall what she said. It was just her pain poured out through her lips. Perhaps it was just hysterical sounds and no words at all.

Dior was forced to yell over her. "Despite your proclamations of purity, you, like all your kind, want more of the darkness that's already in yourself. You want to become one flesh with it!"

Labeth lashed Dior across the chest. The crack was deafening. A long line of blood ran from the corner of her jaw, jumped to her collarbone, carved down her chest and across her stomach.

Shocked, Labeth dropped the whip and retreated, tripping on the step out of the circle and falling. She couldn't believe what she'd done. It was like the mirror of who she was had been cracked down the center. This wasn't who she was. The disconnect was so painful she knew she wouldn't be able to live with it.

As Dlanacen moved to take the whip, Dior yelled at Labeth, "Pick it up!" She spat blood at her foot. "Labeth, my bird, discovers she is not so different, that her self and the dark are not so dissonant." The song flooded her consciousness with that night. Pain. Helpless. Hands invading everywhere. Plugging her ears, she screamed harder than she ever had.

Then it stopped—silence, followed by an awful gurgling sound. Uncurling, she saw that her Jemalgee was forcing his black smoke down Dior's throat, not to possess her host but to choke her. Her host's mouth was opened so unnaturally wide, and blood dripped out of the corner. And that sound. Simultaneously, a sucking and carving of flesh. It was horrific. She hated it. Hated all this bloodshed and pain. Wanted it to stop.

She threw her arms around Dior's torso and cried to her Jemalgee, "Stop it! Please! If you love me, please stop this."

Something shifted beneath her arms, and the Jemalgee pulled away. She retreated as well, not wanting to be touching Dior for another second.

"Why? She deserves this," demanded the Jemalgee.

"But then we are no different than her."

"This is justice!"

"And I want to give mercy!" she screamed, her throat raw from it. "She wants this! Can't you see? She's to be pitied for how lost she is, and we shouldn't let her drag us down with her. Then, she'll have truly won."

The Jemalgee went silent, and Labeth suspected he was trying to read Dior's soul to see if she spoke truth. He didn't resume arguing with her.

Dlanacen turned to the queen. "What do you think, Your Majesty?"

For the first time, Labeth's mother was looking at her with an unfamiliar expression she couldn't read. It wasn't disappointment or exasperation. Her mother wasn't looking at the Labeth she thought she knew but was studying her to see who her daughter truly was. "Nothing changes," she replied. "We'll proceed with banishing it to the Unfound World tomorrow night." And she helped Labeth out of the pit, keeping a gentle arm around her.

"Will you be banishing the vessel too?" asked Labeth.

"We must. We can't risk it escaping."

Labeth didn't like it, but she didn't argue. It was the best option considering the circumstances.

The queen turned to her Jemalgee and did the unthinkable. She thanked him. Labeth didn't understand what could've changed her mother so much, but she didn't press the issue. She was still on thin ice.

"Will you uphold your part of the deal?" the queen asked him.

"Yes. I will leave for the Unfound World with her."

Pain ripped through Labeth's chest. "No," she cried without thinking. "Mother, please don't make him go."

"It is for the best," said the Jemalgee. "I no longer have a place in this world."

Labeth pulled out of her mother's arms to stand close to his cloud of black smoke. "Don't do this. You can't give up." The Unfound World was a place even closer to the Ghustaugness, and most of the Jemalgee had passed over or been banished to it over the last few centuries. No one knew what the effect of being closer to the Ghustaugness had on the creatures because nobody cared as long as they were gone. But Labeth cared. And she feared that the Jemalgee would never find rest if he crossed over.

"I won't," he replied. "Because of you, hope glimmers like the north star over the sea. It will lead me wherever I go. But," he added, "though I may admire it, that light is not mine to have for it would die at my touch. You have seen the corruption of my kind and what a danger I am to you."

"I know you would never hurt me," she said without hesitation. There was no need to consider it. It was a truth she knew in her deepest part.

A ripple raced through the wall of black smoke, and the Jemalgee was silent for several moments. One tendril of smoke reached out to cup her cheek, and she placed her hand over it. At the physical touch, they touched souls, and the Jemalgee saw all the pain, despair, and self-hatred she'd been experiencing.

"It's taken over thousands of years, but you've shown me tonight that the purest light is not what never knew the taste of darkness but that which was drowned in its stream and still chose to crawl out. Not only that, but you showed mercy to your torturer—something I have never seen done. Your heart shines true no matter what Dior has done to you. You are beautiful and pure of heart as always."

His words made her cry. Because of their connection, he knew exactly what she needed to hear, and he didn't lie. The comfort of his praise was inexplicable after all the beatings she'd endured by the hands of her self-hatred. She would hold onto those words forever.

Withdrawing, he slipped out of the temple and into the night.

When Labeth returned to her rooms, Sorsetha was waiting to help her undress. She complied but ordered her to leave after. Taking a candle to her desk, she gathered the ripped pages and thrown journals. She smoothed out their pages and pieced the ripped ones together, mending the broken bones of the letters and lines, and began copying them into a new journal.

Ilsaphanor

Captain Reyoth exited his cabin to take his nightly stroll over his ship's deck. He would pace across every floor board and inspect every knot, not because he was worried about his ship's integrity—he trusted his crew—but he needed something to whittle the night away since he could never sleep. Ever since the beginning of the war, it had eluded him. Loreiak had had peace for several decades; Captain Reyoth's father had fought in the last one as a young man and now he was senile and old. Reyoth paid a maid to take care of him since his mother had passed several years before. He'd been a naval man, and Reyoth had followed in his footsteps and had even superseded him to become captain of the *Wave Breaker* in the Queen's Navy.

But he had rarely seen any bloodshed. Most of his job entailed patrolling the seas along Loreiak's border, keeping the ship in top shape, and apprehending the occasional pirate. Ever since he'd been expected to do the true purpose of his position—sink enemy ships and kill their sailors—an uneasiness had taken hold of him so that he couldn't sleep and on rare occasions even felt seasick. It was shameful that the captain of the ship would turn out to be a yellow-bellied wuss. He hid it as best he could.

The yellow lights of the city Ilsaphanor shown through the fog like a beetle's eyes. It was the quietest part of the night, and always seemed to Reyoth to be the longest and most tedious to get through. He wished for dawn. He loved the way the light played on the sea where it met the horizon.

He nodded to the helmsman on duty as he passed but didn't say a word. A few moments later, the helmsman called out to him. He turned and—the whole ship jerked back and forth, the movement wild and sudden enough to make most men seasick. If he hadn't been on ships his whole life, Reyoth would've fallen on his belly. He grabbed onto the nearest shroud in case it happened again.

"What was that?" the helmsman exclaimed. He'd fallen off the barrel he'd been sitting on and wasn't able to regain his feet before the ship's prow, pointing toward the sea, exploded. Something crashed into Reyoth's face, and he saw red, sky, spinning. He was on the deck, his face kissing the wood. A loud ringing drowned out everything else, and Reyoth felt sluggish and clumsy when trying to move. Everything was a blur. What was happening?

The helmsman stood in his line of vision, his mouth wide like he was screaming, but Reyoth could only hear a muffled, "Abandon ship!" The other man shook Reyoth's shoulders, and his mouth repeated the motion of the words. Somehow, the captain found his feet again, and they dove over the railing.

The water's chill shocked him from his stupor. The helmsman was no longer holding on to him. He was no longer a captain; his ship was gone. It was every man for himself.

He pulled himself onto the dock, flopping around like a fish. Everything was in chaos—screaming, booms, and the cracking of wooden ships. Above it all, the lighthouse passed its eye over the scene and extended it out into the sea. Several oblong shapes broke the surface of the water like the backs of whales, but columns stuck out of their heads and cannons spewed from their mouths. Reyoth grasped for their name. It had been whispered in fear around him enough times.

Submarines.

The Toa were attacking.

They blew the dock to pieces before dispatching small boats that moved faster than wind could push. They landed on the beach before the city of Ilsaphanor could organize a defense, and the soldiers had rifles and small balls that exploded with the force of cannons when thrown. The Loreiakians' swords were no match. They fell before the Toa's superior technology like they had in many battles prior. The best weapons they had were the cannons in the city's fort. But they were slow to load compared to guns and weren't as precise. They caused as much damage to their own city as to the Toa's soldiers.

Seeing their city fall to fire and force, they gave a messenger the town's fastest steed and their hopes that their queen would avenge them—and maybe they would live to see it. Digging his heels into the horse, the messenger left his city behind. Left behind the disfigured buildings. Left behind the young men to be rounded up and killed. Left the women and children screaming and crying into what was usually the quietest part of the night. Left a naval captain to float face-down in the water in the endless sleep.

Dior

I COULDN'T STOMACH TO LOOK OUT of my cell's bars at the people below since I couldn't sense their souls like I always could have. It's like not being able to breathe for our kind (YOU DID THIS TO ME. REDUCED ME TO A HUMAN). They are all stupid, especially that girl. How can she know anything when she can't even touch a soul!

They kept me in a stone prison, high up in the cliffs of Mt. Jakor, and I had been forced to *walk*. My feet hurt, and my human prison was fighting the urge to relieve itself. There was no pan. It smelled like decade old sewage. Never been cleaned. I hope you're happy about what you've done to me, lenou-chaser. (I hope you remember).

They could keep me in a prison miles above their city; they could keep me locked in a vessel, but nothing would have made those fools safe. I didn't know if it would work, but I would rather truly die than to let you get away with this.

When I smashed my vessel's head against the iron bars, the pain was extraordinary (THIS IS WHAT YOU'VE DONE TO ME) for we've experienced very little pain in the last several centuries. We've pursued pleasure for so long. I thought of you and smashed the vessel's head till the face caved in and the body crumpled.

The guards tried to stop me, but they were useless as always. How could they retaliate? Kill me?

VII

A figurine of the Toa flag—a blue background with a white bear—sat on the map of Loreiak over Ilsaphanor, not more than a day's ride from Soros Cereminir. Labeth couldn't take her eyes off of it. It was unthinkable. She couldn't grasp how this was happening. Her country was at war, and they were losing.

It was only the day after she'd faced down Dior in the Temple of Blood. She'd felt lighter since the previous night, as she had won a small victory over herself, but fear was pulling her down again.

She sat on a bench at the edge of the room with Reshelia beside her and Asanilph standing at her elbow. The situation was so dire that their mother had wanted all of her daughters to know what was going on. Servants had carried in the bench and insisted that Reshelia sit for the meeting even though she wasn't far enough along in her pregnancy to require rest. Labeth had elected to sit with her as much for her sister's comfort as for her own. Their sweaty hands never loosened their grip on each other's.

All of the highest ranking military officers who had been in the city stood around the map with the queen along with a star seer. "The Toa will have to regroup after the attack before heading here," said one officer with a thick brown beard. "They'll take this opportunity to seize total control over Ilsaphanor and establish it as a point for ferrying supplies for the siege."

The siege. Those words unveiled a whole new realm of dread. She'd heard the stories of people starving within the walls of their homes and resorting to eating rats.

"Are there troops to the East we could pull back to help fortify Soros Cereminir?" asked her mother.

The bearded officer pressed his lips together. "We're spread thin, Your Majesty. If we pull back any troops to help, we'll lose those cities."

"We are already surrounded," said another officer. "We have to protect the capital. If the capital falls, then all of Loreiak falls."

"If we let other cities fall into their hands in an effort to protect the capital, we won't be able to sustain ourselves. They'll be no more Loreiak left to save. We'll be forced to surrender."

"Maybe we should consider surrendering," said the third officer. He'd been standing silently across the table from Labeth's mother with arms crossed and face unreadable for most of the meeting. Now, he looked to the queen. "We are grossly underprepared to meet this threat. Their technological advancements allow them to slaughter us, and it's been shown to us many times how unprepared we are for this type of threat. No amount of troops will withstand their guns and bombs. I hate to admit it, my Queen, but I think there's no way we can defeat them."

Her mother lowered her gaze to the figurines on the board, not saying a word. Labeth wondered how could he say that. She almost called him traitor. It was unthinkable to let the country she had known her whole life, the country she was born to lead, fall into the enemy's hands. She wanted to give another suggestion but couldn't think of one. She hoped that was just because of her inexperience with war.

"They might have demands," the officer continued. "If we meet them, they could show mercy."

No, no, no! This was so wrong. The Toa had already slaughtered thousands of her people so easily and carelessly. They were greedy and would not be kind rulers. They were not worthy of Loreiak.

Her mother straightened, preparing to answer.

Labeth rushed to the table. "We can't surrender! Our people are counting on us. To do more than hope for mercy from people who have never given it. For their sake, we can't give up on Loreiak. We're not worthy of this country if we don't risk everything we have to protect it."

Everyone stared at her dumbstruck, and Labeth began to wonder if she should have restrained herself. She rarely said anything in war meetings because she assumed people wouldn't respect her opinion. She probably would have embarrassed her mother like she usually did. She'd probably done it now. Labeth kept her eyes lowered and turned away from the queen.

The queen's next words were for the star seer. "What do the stars say of our chances?"

"I'm afraid their message is very grim, Your Majesty. But not hopeless. They speak of some great force that could tip the scales. But it was hard to read. It was shrouded in darkness," he said.

A long moment of silence stretched, everyone leaned toward the queen in expectation. "We will fight," she finally said.

Labeth lifted her eyes to meet her mother's and was met, for the first time, with pride.

"The stars say there is a chance and my daughter is right. We will not hand over our country so easily," she said, holding Labeth's gaze.

"Yes, my Queen," said the officer who had suggested surrender.

They continued drafting battle strategies for the next hour. Labeth kept her spot at the table, listening carefully and giving what small suggestions she could. Her mother never interrupted her or seemed exasperated by her contributions. Each time her mother considered her words, Labeth's confidence grew.

Once everyone else had been dismissed, the queen approached her daughters and kissed each one on the brow. Labeth was grateful but at the same time scared. Was she only doing this because she feared it would be one of the last times she could? A part of Labeth wanted her to act normal, like nothing was wrong, so maybe it could be that way.

"This will not be easy," her mother said. "Stay strong." And she left.

Asanilph disappeared without a word, so Labeth walked with Reshelia down the hallway to the west wing where their rooms were. To their right was a endless row of stained glass windows that stretched all the way down the long hallway. Each depicted a different piece of nature—a rose, a mountain, a tree, a bird—framed by clear glass so one could see the city below.

"Do you think we can win?" ask Reshelia so quietly Labeth had to tilt her head to hear.

"We have to." That answer wasn't enough, but it was the only one she had.

They continued on in silence till a loud boom like thunder shook the chandeliers. They exchanged a look, too frightened to speak. Were the Toa already here?

Labeth peeked out of the clear glass and saw a large cloud of dust rising around the Celestial. The monument also looked different, but she couldn't figure out why. Above the Temple District leered a huge cloud of black smoke. Even from this far, Labeth recognized it.

Dior!

It was better to ask for forgiveness than permission. Labeth had plenty of practice with that method, so she didn't hesitate to steal a horse from the stables. As the crown princess, they were all hers, so it wasn't technically stealing. She rode down to the Temple District, leaving all guards behind. She didn't even think about them following her or slowing down to let them catch up.

She had to get to the Temple District. She had to stop Dior. Details would come later.

People were flooding out of the district's gates when she arrived. Many wept or cried out in shock, and others cradled wounded limbs or bloody cuts. Dust filled the air and irritated Labeth's eyes and nose. There was no way to fight against the outpouring of people on horseback without hurting someone, so she dismounted and shoved her way inside. Things were so chaotic that no one recognized her.

Inside the district, carts and cages had been abandoned and the animals had broken loose. They had shit everywhere out of fright. People lay on the ground, struck down by flying debris. Labeth meant to help them but froze when she saw what had caused the destruction. Dior had broken one of the pillars of the Celestial into pieces and tossed it down onto the Temple District like a kid throwing a rag doll. Now that it was on the ground, Labeth could see how massive it was. It was three times her height and just as wide—an impressive feat done by her ancestors. It knocked the breath out of her to see something so big, so magnificent, an anchor of her nation's pride, toppled. She stared at it several moments in shock, forgetting why she had come.

Another boom rattled the ground. Above, two gargantuan clouds of black smoke twisted through the air. One had just thrown the other against the side of Mt. Vashilien causing an avalanche of rocks that smashed into temples and people. A new chorus of screams burrowed into Labeth's ears. There was so much going on it was overwhelming.

A nearby cry woke her from her trance. A man was waving at her from the ground, for a large stone had fallen on his legs. She rushed to lift it, but it was too heavy. The man grabbed her dress and screamed something unintelligible at her.

"I'm sorry! I'm trying!" she yelled back, panicking.

The guards who had followed her finally caught up. One helped her lift the stone, another carried the man to safety, and the others she ordered around to help get everyone out. She ran to the fallen pillar. Blood stained its underside. She dared not look at it too long. She wanted to scream, but she had to stay focused.

She and the guards worked on unburying the people who were still alive and navigating them to safety. When another rumble shook everything and rocks again fell from the sky, a guard pulled her behind the lone remaining wall of a temple. Once the worst of that avalanche had passed, she peeked out at the Celestial. The two Jemalgee fought dangerously close to another pillar, nearly knocking it down. She knew neither of them would give up. All of Soros Cereminir would be destroyed before that would happen.

She ran toward the stairs up to the monument, ducking away from the guard who tried to stop her. Since the pillar had fallen to the right of the stairs, they were mainly untouched except for some small boulders obstructing the way. When she reached the center of the monument, the sky was completed covered by the fighting Jemalgee, their smoky forms blacker than the darkest thunderstorm. They churned like a maelstrom, and around her, it seemed as if it was night. It was cold, and wind whipped her hair around.

It was then that she realized: what was she going to do? What could she do? She had no strength or powers with which to stop the most powerful beings this earth had known. She was useless, a reality she feared, but she just had to do something.

She started calling her Jemalgee, screaming at him to take Dior away before they caused more damage. Within a minute, her throat felt raw. She gave it all she had and prayed to the universe that this would stop.

The maelstrom of smoke slowed and began to part in the middle like a sky clearing. Even the wind died down.

The Jemalgee's smoke was so entangled she couldn't tell them apart. One slowly pulled further out of the other's grasp and seemed to rear what was its head to look down at her. She thought it must be her Jemalgee at first, but just as she realized it wasn't, it lunged at her. It was so fast Labeth hadn't had time to flinch before Dior was shoving herself down her throat. All the darkness of the maelstorm—the cold, the wind, the helplessness—crashed into her and spread like smoke to fill all of her spirit. The loss of control was instant. She only had her eyes to see the column of smoke burrowing into her mouth.

Her Jemalgee grabbed the rest of Dior's form still outside of her and pulled. Dior didn't stop, and Labeth feared nothing could save her. But then the darkness inside her began to retreat. It was as if she had been drowning and the water was being pulled out of her lungs. Once all of Dior was out, Labeth collapsed onto the ground, unable to do anything but breathe. Sweet air. What once had felt to her nothing was now for a moment everything.

Her Jemalgee pulled Dior out of the Celestial into the sky above the Temple District. They tumbled around each other. Their gargantuan forms displaced the air, stirring up a hurricane-like wind. Labeth buried her face in her arms to protect her eyes from the dust. The rustling of the trees was deafening. It felt like a storm coming, and her whole body warned her to seek shelter, but it was too late.

She forced her head up in time to see the Jemalgee crash into Lake Urvuspha on the other side of the city. The wave created by their impact was what Labeth imagined the Toa's explosions looked like. Its tip stretched to be level with her at the Celestial—the highest point of the city—and its waters flooded the lakeside beach and the buildings on its edge.

As the flood waters retreated, the wind died down, and there were no more great waves. The Jemalgee had disappeared beneath the lake's surface. Where had they gone?

Another wave exploded from the lake's center, and Dior flew out of the water. Labeth braced for another attack, but the Jemalgee fled into the mountains. Labeth sighed in relief. It was over. But seeing the destruction to her city beneath her belied that there was much more still to do.

She stood just as her Jemalgee emerged from the lake, slowly so as not to create another destructive wave. Labeth called to him, and though they were miles apart, he came to her, settling around her as softly as mist. There were so many things she wanted to say. What happened? What were they going to do about Dior? Thank you for saving not only her life but her soul. But there was something that was more pressing than all that.

"Please, there's people trapped under the pillar. Can you move it?"

He didn't even reply but went immediately to help. She raced down the steps after him, and together along with the guards and doctors, they rescued many people and carried them to a nearby hospital. Upon seeing the Jemalgee so close, all the people being rescued screamed in horror, but the Jemalgee continued helping without a word.

Eventually, Labeth's mother arrived at the Temple District with a whole host of guards and a collection of priests. They had no eyes for the destruction or the dead; their gazes were locked on the Jemalgee. Her mother's face was unreadable, but Dlanacen looked furious. As he began chanting, Labeth stepped forward to stop him.

"He's helping!" she said.

"He caused this!" Dlanacen replied, his face so red with rage that a vein pulsed at his temple.

"It was the other one. She escaped, and he fought her to protect us!"

"I will go," came the rumbling voice of the Jemalgee behind her.

Labeth turned to him and with the authority of a queen told him no. "You are more than the darkness everybody says you are." To all she said, "He, a creature you've said has every inclination toward evil, has done so much good today. He's protected this city from being destroyed and rescued many who would've died without his help. We will not send him away like some pest."

"Girl," said Dlanacen, "you are fooling with things that will destroy you."

"I think I understand things better than you ever have." She was so sick of people condescending to her and not understanding what was so clear. She thought that after seeing the Jemalgee help them, people would recognize the goodness struggling to stay alive in him. "Where were you and the other priests while he helped us? You ran away from your people when you are the only ones with the power to protect us from the Jemalgee."

Dlanacen began to reply, but her mother said, "Enough." And of course he obeyed her.

"We need to take the wounded to the hospital and start clearing the debris. There will be no more fighting between the two of you," her mother said. "But," she looked over Labeth's shoulder at the Jemalgee, "he may go. We can handle the rest."

There was no contempt in her voice, only a calm finality. Somehow, it ceased the fight in Labeth—maybe it was some queenly power which Labeth hoped to possess. She turned to the Jemalgee and mouthed to him, *Meet me in the cave tonight.* She didn't want this moment to be the last time she saw him nor could she say what she wanted to with the people watching. A familiar tingle ran through her as he touched her soul and read her intentions, and then he flew away into the mountains. The collective relief at the Jemalgee's departure from everyone else was permeable. Labeth felt only sadness.

After, the people resumed working—the priests helping this time—but Labeth's mother took her arm and led her to the carriage she had arrived in. It would've taken the queen much longer to reach the Temple District in that than on the horse Labeth had taken, though it was the more dignified way. She wondered if time would cause her to value the dignity suitable for a queen over speed. There were so many things she envied about her mother, but this wasn't one of them. But did people not respect her because she did not choose the dignified way? Hopefully, there was a way to change their minds about that.

Inside the carriage, it was surprisingly dark, the curtains drawn for privacy. Labeth stared at her hands, silent, waiting for a lecture but poised to defend her choices.

"What is it you are looking for in that Jemalgee?" asked her mother calmly.

"What?" Labeth looked up at her in surprise. Her tone wasn't dripping with disgust or horror for once when speaking about the Jemalgee.

"Why are you drawn to it? What do you see?"

Finally, someone bothered to hear her speak about all of this. She'd never expected that person would've been her mother. "The night when we first met, before I fell off of the cliff, we. . .connected in a way that I've never felt before. I could feel his soul and how much he longs to be good. To return to the stars where he's meant to be. He was also so hopeless." Her emotions shifted back to how she had felt that moment. "I didn't know that depth of despair could exist. It is even deeper than the fear we know now that the Toa are on our doorstep." And that fear was very deep.

"It's unspeakable," she went on. No words could ever be enough without the emotion that only the Jemalgee had the ability to truly spill into another person. "No creature should suffer like that. Not when there's still a part of them wanting redemption.

"I intended to not seek him out again, but when Reshelia got sick, he was my only hope."

Her mother's demeanor shifted, her eyes narrowing. Labeth and her sisters had never revealed the true source of Reshelia's recovery. She revealed everything now, and her mother continued to surprise her by not bursting into parental and queenly fury.

"I know I've made a mess of things," she said but didn't clarify what exactly. She still couldn't speak much about what Dior had done to her. "I only wanted to help him."

"But how could you help it? It is a creature of darkness," her mother stated factually, no venom.

"I thought of a ritual," she replied, the words slipping out before she could consider them. Now that the confession had started, it was hard to stop it before its completion. "Humans have equal capacity for both good and evil. Everyone knows that. If we joined together—not a possession—but a true joining of souls and body, then I believe my goodness could spread to him and redeem him."

Several long moments of silence passed, and her mother was unreadable, especially in the shadows of the carriage. She seemed so distant, and Labeth had never felt more vulnerable. Her soul had been read by two Jemalgee, but she'd never felt in a more precarious position of judgment by someone she had desired respect from her whole life. This would be the nail in the coffin. Her mother would cast her out for her lunacy.

"You really believe that it would work?" her mother asked.

"Yes." Her chest was so tight it was difficult to get the word out.

"Get it to agree, and we'll perform the ritual tomorrow."

Labeth was dumbstruck. She was so thrown she couldn't think of a response for the whole trip back, and when they arrived at the palace, her mother was quickly pulled away by servants.

Her mother had listened to her.

Jemalgee

I THOUGHT ABOUT NOT MEETING WITH YOU that night, and every day since I've regretted not doing so. It would've been the right thing to do for you, but of course, condemned as I am by my nature, I didn't choose what was right.

Dior told me as we fought in the sky about how you intended for yourself to be my host. Again, the depth of your love strikes me like a dying man awakened by the hope of life. I cannot resist it—for long. I try and I try and I try to beat myself with the memory of every horror that has seeped from me to ruin everything else. I am a snake with no control over my venom. It destroys even what I mean to love.

That night in the cave, when you told me your mother had approved and that we could perform the ritual the next night, I told you that you couldn't handle the weight. It would drive you mad (Why didn't you listen to me? Why did I listen to myself?) I would destroy what I love most about you because you are the exact opposite of what I am.

You have eyes that light up not from within, but the light you see, you capture in them. Every drop.

I made the mistake of looking up from your face at the stars. Nothing on this earth and beyond can compare to the bliss of living among them. Completeness. Balance. No pain. I feel it in the threads of my soul that was stitched to be among them. I have never wanted anything more than to return to them. Maybe there was a chance, a possibility you were right (I tricked myself into thinking).

You said there was good in me, and I agreed to try. But even my quest for redemption was swaddled in selfishness.

You paid the price.

And I will never be redeemed of that destruction.

VIII

"The ritual has been prepared to your specifications, Your Highness." High Priest Dlanacen bowed his head in reference, but Labeth heard the disdain in his voice. Her mother had informed him and the other priests of Labeth's plan without her present, and she hadn't heard a word of criticism come out of the high priest's mouth. She wondered what her mother had said to get him to agree.

Did it matter? She'd finally earned the respect of her mother and people were listening to her now. It felt good. After this, her people would no longer have to fear all Jemalgee and instead could work with them. And her Jemalgee's suffering would end. Maybe more after him could be turned.

Labeth, her mother, the priests, and some guards were gathered in the Celestial. Even before Dior's escape, Labeth had decided that this ritual could not be done in any place less sacred than the Celestial. Its pillars contained a different energy, but it felt disrupted now that one of them was lost.

Priests bustled around from every corner, fixing this and that to be perfected for the ritual. In the center of the Celestial was a circle plated in silver that glittered in the lantern light, and in its center was a small sphere of diamond. Acolytes encircled the larger one in chalk and placed candles at the northeast, southeast, southwest, and northwest points. By each candle was a small d-ring set into the stone where chains would be connected. This wouldn't be the first time a person was the center of a dangerous ritual here.

"Are you sure the ritual will work?" her mother asked once Dlanacen had left them.

"I've done my research. It will." She pressed all of her confidence into her voice so her mother wouldn't doubt. Labeth didn't like to think of it not working and the resulting embarrassment. She'd just gained some respect; she couldn't lose it. But she had done her research and it should work. Just in case, there would be a safeguard in the ritual that would protect her from the oil and fire that would be involved, so even if it didn't work, she would not be harmed.

She told her mother she'd be ready in a minute and stepped out of the Celestial onto the rocky mountainside. Immediately, it became much darker and colder. She shivered in the silk robe she was wearing. But a few moments later, she felt the night shift, and a tingle traced her cheek like a caress. He was here.

"Are you certain?" came a whisper on the wind.

"Yes," she breathed. Some of the night's darkness flew upward, and a string of black began circling the tops of the pillars.

As she turned to reenter the Celestial, someone cried out behind her. A very pregnant Reshelia struggled up the steep mountain steps toward her. Labeth raced down to meet and steady her, so she wouldn't trip and fall.

"What are you doing here?" she asked her sister.

"Mother told us what you're doing. I can't believe she's letting it happen. It's insane!" Reshelia was speaking quickly. "I didn't say anything before because I didn't want to disobey. If she had decided, then. . .please, don't do this."

Labeth was so surprised she couldn't create a coherent thought for several moments. "Why are you saying this?" Tears already began to prickle her eyes.

"Because I can't lose you too. I need you." As Labeth tried to reassure her, Reshelia continued, her words rushing out. "It's still so hard. Everyday. I need you with me—to help me raise her." She nodded toward her belly.

Labeth cupped her cheek. "Don't worry. I'll still be here. That's not going to change."

"You don't know what it'll do to you."

"I can't abandon him. He deserves a second chance, and if I can give that to him, how can I do nothing?"

"Stop trying to save everyone!" Reshelia seized her hands and squeezed them. "You'll destroy yourself."

"If it weren't for him, you'd be dead."

"I know, I'm thankful. I see what you mean, that he is different. But this is too far. You don't owe him this."

"But I'm going to give it to him anyway because that's what's right. It's what I'm meant to do."

"No," Reshelia told her like a queen giving orders. "You're supposed to be queen and to lead your people. You're not meant to go off to save something else. Your people need you."

"I'm doing this for them." Labeth had thought she'd finally been gaining ground with helping people to see things the way she did, so she didn't understand why her sister was fighting with her. Of all people, she should've been the one to understand the most since the Jemalgee had healed her. "So they may know that nothing is ever so lost it can't be found again. I felt so hopeless—too many times—when I saw everything that was wrong with this world and that it kept winning. We have to fight. And if the deepest darkness can be made pure again, we can do anything."

Reshelia's grip on her hands went limp as she pulled away, tears in her eyes. "You don't know that."

"I have faith. It's going to be okay." She pulled Reshelia into a hug, but her sister didn't lean into it and only gave her back the lightest of touches. Labeth drew away, more isolated than before. "I'll get a guard to walk you down to make sure you don't trip. You should be back at the palace resting."

They parted in awkward silence, and Labeth felt less confident than before. She still wanted to go through with it, but it hurt that her sister hated the decision. She wasn't leaving her. She loved Reshelia. Would do anything for her—except abandon what she thought was right. Her sister would come around eventually. She'd prove it to her like she would to everyone.

When Labeth reached the Celestial, she told the first guard she saw to help her sister back to the palace. Before he went, he thanked her for intervening during the Jemalgee's attack and helping them save the wounded. She broke into a huge smile that she couldn't make dignified. She was sure her response was nothing like that of a queen, but she was so happy to hear his words. She didn't want to be a distant leader like her mother, and someone had recognized that as a good thing.

She thanked him and approached the center of the Celestial now that the priests were done setting everything up. Attached to two of the d-rings were chains—one for each arm. It was for her protection so she would not injure herself or others if she convulsed. Their edges had either rusted or been stained with the dried blood of people who had been sacrificed when the practice had been more popular. Once she slipped out of her silk robe and revealed her naked body, an acolyte clamped her wrists in the chains. She wanted to cross her arms to hide her nudity. No one dared stare at her, but she still focused on a stone in front of her to hide her discomfort.

Next, the acolyte poured sand and oil over her. It clung to her hair and dripped into her eyes and her mouth. She had to refrain herself from spitting out the muddy mixture. The acolyte poured the oil along a path from her to the edge of the Celestial.

Her mother and the guards retreated so far into the shadows that Labeth could no longer see them. There were only the priests in their hooded robes, one standing in the gap between each pillar. Incense tickled her nose.

The priests began to chant.

Labeth tilted her head back to watch the Jemalgee waiting for his time to enter her. Past him shone a million stars that glistened against the dust of the sky. It was an enchanting mixture of purple, black, and indigo. The stars were so beautiful and distant. No matter what she did, she'd never be able to reach them. Hopefully, this would work, and he would be able to return to them.

She sang to the stars:

> "May pride and pain be put away tonight
> and may your schism again be melded tight
> as with this strange new bond we seek to grow
> the light lost in what seemed eternal sorrow."

A priest lit the oil, and the flames flared so bright that Labeth had to close her eyes. The heat rushed toward her, and just as the first lick of fire burned her, she felt the Jemalgee swoop in through her screaming mouth just as Dior had done. The physical pain was replaced with something worse—a tearing of her deepest part, her soul. She convulsed in agony, hitting her shoulders, knees, and head against the stone so hard they throbbed.

The Jemalgee's presence was heavy. Overwhelming. His being, so vast it could spread from the furthermost corners of Loreiak, filled her soul. Pain, sorrow, hope, beauty, and darkness roiled inside her. She screamed, but as the joining finished, her cries turned into a beautiful singing wail that echoed through the Celestial and off the mountains. It sent shivers into everyone who heard it as their ears were assaulted by something otherworldly and that contained such extreme grief.

The oil and sand mixture coating her transformed into glass that slid off as she struggled. Gradually, she stilled as the Jemalgee rose to the surface of their joined consciousness. Again, they looked to the stars and sang:

> "Forgive me the mistake of wanting when
> I needed nothing in your company.
> When first I walked in human feet, immense
> mouths yawned inside where lust and gluttony,
>
> the wrath and pride, sensation so intense
> burned me to a crisp and left me hungry.
> Forgive me! May her mercy ease my torment,
> so I may lie once again in your elegance—."

Their voice faded as they sensed Dior was near. Above, the stars one by one blinked out as a pool of impenetrable darkness slid over the sky, staining it black. They felt the familiar, disgusting touch of her soul and remembered the threat she'd spoken the first night Labeth had mentioned the ritual to him: *If you try it, I'll make sure that you'll never lie in the stars' presence again.*

All across Loreiak, Dior spread her smoky form over the sky, so no one, not even a Jemalgee, could see the stars' beauty. The already dark night became as black and sticky as pitch. People everywhere closed their shutters and wrapped themselves in blankets in an effort to shield themselves from the wrongness coating the land. A Jemalgee's true form was larger than the mountains, so Dior could spread herself thin to make sure nowhere was left untouched.

The little sense Labeth and her Jemalgee had of the stars' presence was ripped away, and it felt as if Labeth's heart had been carved out of her chest. Together, they screamed a beautiful and grotesque wail.

> "No! Why won't you let me any peace! You tear and bite
> at us
> because we cannot dream of anything other than being
> damned!"

They slumped down onto the ground, dizzy and shaken. The priests around them began to shout, but they didn't hear any more as the world became dark.

IX

When day broke, the sun never came, but the bombs did.

Queen Anallia thought the chill that had come over her when the stars blinked out would fade at the touch of a new dawn. Her mother had always told her that no matter how bad things got, a new day was a new start. She had held on to that mantra her whole life. Until now. A new day would not alleviate any part of this monstrosity.

It had still been as dark as night when the bell towers chimed 7 o'clock. The people had gathered in the streets confused and claimed that the bell-ringers were off, but the bell-ringers said they weren't wrong. It wasn't until the day started to brighten a little, though the sun remained hidden, that people went ballistic. It didn't take long for the first person to claim it was the end times; that's when the rioting began. While some stole food from the market and boarded up their homes, others ran to the Temple District to make sacrifices but found the gates closed.

Anallia could see it all from her tower's balcony in the palace. She was ordering her guards to go out and calm the people, cursing that she was sending them to deal with this when the Toa were at their doorstep, and that's when they heard it. A rhythmic thumping and a whine that couldn't come from any human or animal on the earth. It was so loud.

An explosion shook the world, and someone shoved Anallia inside so hard she fell. A guard barred the doorway to the balcony, staring out at the city. His back was tense, and he stayed so still for so long, Anallia thought his mind had gone dead.

"It. . . It fell from the sky, Your Majesty," he finally said.

"The dungeons," said one of the generals.

The dungeons were the only underground part of the palace and weren't used as often as the ones beneath the Temple District. They let anyone who could make it to the palace in through the gates and set up shelters in the dungeons. After only a few hours, the shelters began to overflow into the first floor of the palace since there were so many people. More and more bombs fell, and people came with injuries from the explosions—crushed legs, concussions, punctured lungs, large scrapes and bruises. Anallia had never seen so much covered in blood, and she'd been audience to many sacrifices.

The servants had carried a rug into one large cell where the queen, her daughters, and their guards waited, sheltered from the others. They'd even carried down two small beds for her two eldest daughters. Reshelia, six months pregnant, grimaced in pain as the baby kicked, jostled by its mother's stress. Asanilph knelt beside her, squeezing her hand and trying to calm her. It was too early. If Reshelia went into labor, the baby would die.

Anallia would lose another one.

In the other bed, Labeth lay inert. She hadn't stirred since fainting during the ritual. Anallia sat on the edge of the bed and took one of her hands in hers.

She would probably never wake. It was wise to assume the worse when Jemalgee were concerned. It had been stupid, a desperate scheme. Anallia chuckled bitterly at herself. A scheme for her daughter's life. She hadn't told Labeth this, but when she saw the destruction the two Jemalgee had caused at the Temple District, she thought that maybe Labeth could harness their power to fight off the Toa—that this was what the star seer had meant. She knew that Labeth's plan was dangerous and might even kill her, but she was willing to risk her daughter's life to save her kingdom. It had seemed the only way, because it had been. Now she would lose her kingdom too.

Labeth limped through a maze of mirrors. It was coming for her. When she'd woken in this strange place, a large, black form had been leering over her. She hadn't gotten a good look at it, because just the glimpse of it had seized her with terror. She had immediately turned and run. Its jaw clamped down on the back of her left leg, and she kicked and thrashed till it let go. She could feel that a chunk of her calf was missing but didn't dare waste any time to examine it. The blood ran warm down her ankle, leaving a nice trail for it to track her by, though she had a feeling that it didn't need that to find her. Its shadow touch was always at her back.

All the mirrors extended fifty feet or more into the air and stood at odd angles with no rhyme or reason to them. Everywhere she looked, her frightened face stared back at her. There wasn't even a way to see where one mirror began or another ended because every one reflected all the others, so she was endlessly lost in multiple dimensions. She leaned on them, navigating by touch to somewhere. She had no destination because she couldn't see one. She just needed to get away.

Labeth flinched at a loud, sharp crash, causing her to trip and fall. Above, the black monster had shattered the top half of a mirror and its pieces fell like glittering snow. It tore through another and another, and with each broken mirror, something stabbed into her chest. She pounded at it, but there was nothing to defend against.

When she couldn't stand again, she crawled. The black monster jumped in front of her, and she turned her face away, shielding her head with her hands. Its warm breath pressed against her in huffs like a horse. Moments stretched by like hours while Labeth waited for the monster to eat her. When nothing happened, she looked up into its face.

Its elongated snout contained multiple rows of crooked, yellowed teeth. Its long neck arched over her like a swan's so it could stare her down with its yellow eyes. In-between them were its horns running from the crown of its head to the end of its tail. They looked deathly sharp and jagged, though they moved and flexed like feathers. Its body was long like a snake's, and its leathery skin clung so tightly to its thin frame that it looked emaciated. Three sets of webbed wings protruded from its back, but they blended together to create the illusion of one pair of massive wings. The first set curled above its head, coming to thin ends like horns. The second were wider and stuck further from its sides, and the third set were long and extended as far out from it as its body was long. They made it look like a massive bat leering over her.

A memory of seeing a wall painting of this creature flashed into her mind. She hadn't been scared then, only curious, because it had been a Jemalgee. It had been him.

"You," she breathed. This must be what his body looked like when it wasn't smoke, except in a much smaller form.

She extended her hands forward, palms up, and he sniffed at them before nuzzling his snout against them. "There, there," she said softly. "I'm sorry I ran from you." He didn't reply, and she found it odd that he didn't speak to her.

Instead, he pulled away, his nostrils flaring and breathing black smoke. In his eyes was an intensity that was indecipherable from lust or the strongest hate.

For the first time, she felt afraid.

You don't know what it'll do to you.

If you gaze into Darkness, destruction is all you will find.

There's light in you, Creature of Darkness. Don't forget that.

She remembered cupping her sister's cheek. I have faith. It's going to be okay. She'd come this far. She wasn't going to back down now. Steeling herself, she pushed her hands closer to him. "Come to me."

He lunged, leaping into her mouth and pouring down her throat so fast she couldn't even choke or gag. His movement was as swift and powerful as the ocean's waves, pummeling her down. When he finally disappeared into her, she went to retch—

And opened her eyes.

The ceiling was made of stone, one she had never seen before. Blurry figures stood in the far off corner and crystallized into her mother and her generals. A high-pitched shout assaulted her ears, and then hands pulled her up and enfolded her. They belonged to her sisters. Their grief and relief stung her double-fold as she sensed it like it was her own, unable to control the intensity. She pulled away still too discombobulated to say anything, and her mind disengaged from her body like she couldn't keep it in.

Far above, on the streets of her city, thousands of soldiers marched their bloody boots on the cobblestones. They pulled people from their homes, shot those who struggled, and burned their houses and possessions. They didn't want any of it, for they only wanted what they weren't destined to have—magic. Greed deafened their ears to the screams and hardened their hearts so no empathy could get in, but all the people's sorrows and pain burrowed into Labeth. They were monsters, but she told herself that nothing was beyond salvation. She'd sacrificed her body and mind to prove that. With the power of a Jemalgee to read and share souls, she would confront them with the sorrow they had caused others, so they would drop their weapons and never take another life. She didn't want any more bloodshed—she hadn't wanted any at all. This would be her chance to turn things around the way she had always wanted to. She could finally do the good she desired.

She ran out of the dungeon without a word. When the guards tried to stop her, Labeth pushed them aside with a wave of black smoke. There was no time to explain. Even now, she felt the turn in the Toa soldier's minds as they looked toward the palace.

She stopped a quarter of the way down the winding path leading from the palace to the city. Large plumes of smoke rose to the black sky, and the two combined made it seem all of Soros Cereminir was trapped in a dark cave, quickly becoming unbreathable. The acrid fumes made her cough. And the blood red flames in the city stood lurid against the dark.

The soldiers were just now starting up the road. Within their ranks was a large machine that moved like a carriage without any horses. On its top, a cylindrical nozzle extended forward like a crow's beak.

She sang loud enough for the sound to bounce against the five mountains:

> "You come to satisfy your sinful greed,
> but it won't gratify your begging need.
> Your envy and your ego
> lead you into murdering
> the orphan, the widow."

The machine's beak spit out a large metal object that crashed into the cliff above her, shaking the earth so hard it threw her off her feet. Boulders, some as large as horses, tumbled down to her left. Labeth didn't have time to run away. Instinctively, she threw up a hand, and the Jemalgee flew out of her in black smoke to deflectthe boulders that would've crushed her.

She got to her feet and shouted down to the soldiers again:

"Stop this! Lay down and join with me
lest those you kill join your dreams.
Their voices never let go.
Deeds can't be undone—."

When they fired again at her, the Jemalgee snatched the missile from its course and threw it at the soldiers. The ground burst like a volcano, spewing a reddish mixture of blood and dirt and bodies.

It was unbelievable. Not even the truth of a Jemalgee's words could break them from their deadly path. The lengths that people would go to satiate their greed sickened her. Her anger was more than she could've born as a mere human. There was no stopping it, and if she tried to contain it, she would go mad. She screamed.

"How can you rip us to shreds?
Rip, rape, kill till nothing's left!
Deeds can't be undone,
And memories never not know.
May you die by what you sow!"

When they fired again, she transformed fully into the smoke of a Jemalgee, grabbed it, and cast it into their ranks. The Toa had been terrorizing her country for too long. *The Sunbound,* Hithlin, Reshelia, Ilsaphanor had been pummeled into shadows of themselves, and these soldiers knew no remorse. After all the good she and the Jemalgee had been striving for, they still couldn't stop the soldiers from coming. But they wouldn't back down. They would make them stop. It was all a blur. Red, red, red rage, black smoke, and tearing metal. Their wrath poured and poured out of them for what could've been centuries.

Eventually, they'd had to stop, not because the rage was gone, but because there was nothing left to receive it. Labeth woke in her own body surrounded by the soldiers. All dead. They were no longer people but carnage: tall stacks of unattached arms, legs, and torsos; puddles of brain matter and intestines; and the great metal machine had been twisted into a grotesque sculpture that stared down at everything, crushed soldiers stuck between its wheels' treads like teeth.

As horror dawned, she screamed. And screamed. And did not stop.

X

A year later to the day of the Toa's attack, Soros Cerminir celebrated. The people had been busy preparing since the early morning and had hung lanterns everywhere for evening fell fast in the days after the Darkening—the night the sky had been lost to darkness.

After the slaughter, Loreiak had recaptured Ilsaphanor. The queen gave two of the Toa prisoners one of their inventions, a camera, and had made them take pictures of the carnage at Soros Cereminir to carry back with them to their country. She made sure to inform them how this had been done by one person with the power of mysticism. Within the next month, the Toa pulled back all their troops, even from the cities they had occupied for months. There'd been rejoicing in the streets, and the people of Loreiak had been busy building back their country since.

Rumors crept around about what had slaughtered the soldiers. No one doubted that it must have been a Jemalgee. While some hated the idea, the majority were thankful it had saved their lives despite their fear of it. All had known how dire their country's stance in the war had been, and they were glad their country had won, no matter the means.

The real question was how had the crown convinced a Jemalgee to fight for Loreiak. Some who had been in the palace dungeons when it had happened claimed they saw the crown princess shoot black smoke from her hands. The queen made no comment. Many dismissed it as nonsense, but the fact that the crown princess had not made a public appearance in the entire year since only added to the suspicions. It was said that she had been plagued with several illnesses and was unable to rise from bed most days.

But she would make an appearance today. A new monument had been built in the Temple District at her orders, and the crown princess herself would unveil it to the people tonight.

At second nightfall—what would've been true nightfall before the Darkening moved it earlier to what was known as the first nightfall—the procession from the palace to the Temple District began. First came the priests, then the guards, and then the queen and her daughters in a large chariot pulled by eight white horses. People lined the streets, packed so tightly no one could see the ground.

The queen stood at the helm, waving to the crowd, while Asanilph tossed white rose petals that signified victory. Reshelia sat in the middle, holding her nine-month old daughter, Lilira, in her lap. The child giggled at her surroundings. She was the darling of the people in her white dress and with a small curl of blonde hair atop her head.

Beside Reshelia sat Labeth, dressed in a white dress with silky sleeves that looked like water. On her head was a simple ringlet of amethyst encrusted metal. She smiled but didn't join in tossing the petals with Asanilph. She looked thin, her jaw sharper, her eyes darker.

No one had been allowed inside the Temple District for the last week, a very odd occurrence, but once the carriage passed through, the people were allowed to trickle in till there was no more room. The carriage pulled into the small, green field right across from the Celestial's steps. It was at the edge of the district, just outside the line of trees that signaled the beginning of the forest. A sheet covered a small, short, and cylindrical structure. No one knew of its design and purpose. The crown princess, the queen, and the high priest met to stand around it while the other princesses stood to the side with the priests and guards.

Everyone was whispering their suspicions about the monument to each other, so it was impossible to hear anything. Before the musicians could play the trumpets to signal the beginning of her announcement, Labeth opened her mouth and a beautiful voice, unlike anyone on this world, floated from her lips. It stunned everyone silent, and they could do nothing but listen to it, mouths agape in awe. Her voice glided through everyone's soul, taking a small piece of them with it and connecting it to the others it touched. A sense of peace and belonging lay to rest in their hearts, and millions of poems and songs would be written about that day to try in vain to capture its serenity.

Ending the song, the crown princess said, "People of Loreiak, I am pleased to unveil this new monument to not only commemorate our victory over the Toa but to also mark a new era for all of Loreiak."

As she pulled off the sheet, everyone craned their neck to get a closer look.

"It's a well," she said. "A well made of stone from the Fallen Pillar. It is inscribed with an important message I hope we never forget. It is my intention," she continued, "that we revisit this monument on this day every year. It is more than just a well but has special properties that allow it to channel one's energy into light. It would need several humans to truly light this beacon, but it requires only one Jemalgee."

She paused, and the crowd shifted even closer as they hoped the answer to their curiosity was finally arriving.

"I don't want to keep it hidden," she said, "because I am not ashamed. I have been bound to a Jemalgee and I was the one who defended our city from the Toa. But that is not all I intend to do. The Jemalgee was a being tormented and chained to his own ghustaugness, but with my spirit, I will purify him. And I believe his presence can also help us to do many wondrous things—to grow beauty and healing and resilience in all of us." As she said this, she looked to each member of her family.

Stepping forward, she placed her hands on the well and began to sing its inscription:

> "We lay this monument below
> the stars and with the trees and come

here once a year before we plunge
into the future year unknown,

so we may fill this with the flow
of dreams and fears, the eye and brunt
of storms. As light and dark are spun
as one, from earth to heaven grow,

may we recall the strength we know
is first a tale of all our woe."

A beacon of white light shot from the mouth of the well all the way up to the sky. It was terrifyingly beautiful, overwhelming the people with wonder at its power. Like with the crown princess's voice, they couldn't divert their attention from it.

A few moments later, Labeth retreated, and the beacon disappeared. She raised her hands above her head. "Let this be a sign to keep fighting no matter how dark things may appear! We will always find light if we carry on!"

The crowd cheered. Many bowed, weeping and making signs of respect toward Labeth. If anyone expressed their dislike of the crown princess's revelation, they were drowned out by the joy of others.

After the unveiling, the people celebrated more fiercely than they had in years, even more than at Reshelia's wedding. The revelries, the dining, the dancing were at least three times greater than that day.

The queen and her daughters sat on the top step of the main Temple District thruway on small simple thrones while the people celebrated before them. On each large step, people danced in multi-layered circles, entwining and untangling so fast and furiously that it was dizzying to watch. Labeth remembered the last night she'd danced liked that—when she had sneaked away from her sister's wedding with Josa and Osolir. She missed the careless freedom of those days, and she missed her friends. She hadn't seen them or talked to them in the last year. Last she heard, they'd gotten married right after the war. It had happened outside the capital. She'd been invited but not well enough to go.

Labeth had spent the majority of the past year in her room, often in bed, overwhelmed by the darkness she'd accepted. During their night talks, the Jemalgee hadn't elaborated on his past crimes, and Labeth had been more concerned about giving him a future. She heard the tales, had seen the aftermath of the incident the night of Reshelia's wedding, and thought she'd known enough. How naive she'd been. Now that they were one, all of his memories—millennia worth—became her own. The horrors he and his fallen brethren had committed had been beyond her imagination.

And now it seemed that all the darkness of the world was drawn to that inside of her. It'd been ages since she'd been surrounded by this many people because the secrets of their souls always came to her unbidden. She absorbed them like how one, after learning to read, can no longer look at a word and not read it. She used to believe the majority of people were good, but since then, Labeth realized that what was good in them was often a projection like a false face. She knew which ones beat their spouses, who lusted for ones not theirs, and who stirred up trouble because of their envy. She could taste the sweat on the writhing bodies in the whorehouses, hear the faintest rustle of fingers in and out of pockets, and see the jealousies of an invisible girl on another's hold over a boy.

No wine could wash away the bitterness in her mouth at the fact that they were all here to celebrate her slaughter of the Toa. Most of them hadn't seen it, couldn't remember it. It didn't keep them awake at night or haunt them during the day. She'd torn her room apart several times and rocked back and forth in her bed, clawing at the sheets, screaming to drown out the dead soldiers' screams. Few people were allowed to see her after she had pinned several against the walls with the Jemalgee's smoke at the slightest thing that angered her. And everything angered her. She didn't even know why. It was just there. The beast inside of her. The one she'd welcomed.

Some had sought to kill her for being an abomination. She'd reported them, sending them to their deaths, and wondered if maybe she should've let them do it. She tried to push those thoughts away and remind herself why she was doing this. For the last month, she'd been better and hoped the purification was working. Maybe the unveiling of the monument would be the beginning of a new era for not just Loreiak, but for her as well. She and the Jemalgee would be better from now on.

Reshelia handed Lilira to a nurse and tugged on Labeth's hand. "Come on. Let's dance."

"I'm not sure I can." She feared going down into the people.

"I've seen you grow stronger the past month. I know you can," said Reshelia thinking Labeth meant she was too weak to dance. Her sister's eyes pleaded innocently for her to join, but Labeth knew the seed of resentment she hid. She felt abandoned by Labeth and justified that she had been right the night of the ritual and that the joining was causing her to lose her sister. This offer was one of her efforts to drag her sister back into the light.

Should Labeth have listened to her that night?

Feeling guilty, she acquiesced. It took a little to get back in the rhythm of the dance since it had been so long, and she was much weaker than she used to be. She thought no one would want to clasp hands with her, but no one shied away, though their hands were always tense. She read on their souls how they feared offending her. It made Labeth feel more alone than ever. She may follow the movements, but she would never truly be part of a dance again.

In this particular dance was a section where you would partner with one person for an extended period of time. Labeth would've liked to partner with Reshelia, but the dance chose your partner, and she ended up with an acolyte a few years older than she. He had long, dark hair that fell to his shoulders, though the front was pulled back from his face into a small ponytail. He was tall and muscular and had long, thick eyelashes that looked like coal around his eyes.

He bowed his head in respect. "It's a pleasure, Your Highness. I've been wanting to meet you."

His words surprised her. She didn't think anyone wanted to meet the Jemalgee-possessed crown princess. "And who do I have the pleasure of dancing with?"

"My name is Mallinor. I'm the acolyte assigned to your new monument. I wanted to tell you how I will uphold my duty to the utmost importance. It's a wonderful addition."

"That is great to hear. Thank you." In the past, she would've beamed at the prospect of someone believing in her, but now she knew to be wary. She reached out to touch his soul and found that he was genuine, though a bit morbidly curious about her.

But when he spun so her back faced him and he gripped her upper arm, one of his memories pulled her down. A recent one. A fellow acolyte had discovered him stealing from the financial offerings—an act that would get him expelled from the priesthood. Mallinor tried to bribe him to stay quiet, but the boy had been too honorable. So in the heat of rage, Mallinor had shoved him against a wall, cracking his skull and killing him. Blood coated his hand. Blood coated her hands, her whole body, the ground. Piles of broken soldiers she'd torn to shreds. No. NO. It couldn't be. Her chest tightened so much she couldn't breath. She had to escape.

She threw out an arm, and the smoke of the Jemalgee pushed the person away. There was a snap and thud. Labeth collapsed, shaking so much she feared she would break.

She became aware that the ground beneath her fingers was stone, that she was in the Temple District. They were celebrating, but everything was so silent. There was no music, no pounding of feet, no joyous cries or laughter.

Dragging her eyes forward, she saw Mallinor's crumpled body several yards away, his neck at a right angle to the rest of him. His eyes were open and glossy. Pain struck the back of her head, and she knew only darkness.

When Labeth came to, someone was carrying her, and they quickly dropped her. One half of her landed on the edge of the bed and she fell to the floor with a groan. Footsteps rushed away, and the bedroom door slammed shut. Labeth lay there unable to move due to her pounding headache. Reaching back, she felt a small bandage on the back of her head over where she'd been hit. At least they weren't scared enough to not bandage their crown princess up.

She'd killed a man. With a flick of her wrist. He'd been a murderer, but she should not have been his judge and executioner. His memories hadn't been why she'd killed him. It had been hers—the murders she'd done—that she had needed to escape from. Though it wasn't right, she'd done things way worse than his one murder, so how could she punish him for his sins while she roamed free? While she chased redemption?

How merciful she was now, she thought bitterly. She hadn't killed since she'd slaughtered the Toa's army, but at least with that, she could tell herself that she'd given them the chance—that she had had no choice—anything to stay sane, even if she knew it was a lie. But with this? There'd been no such chance.

She was a monster.

Screaming, she pounded the floor, writhing like the insane creature she was. She kicked her bedside table down, pulled off the bed's blankets and sheets, and tore off her jewelry, throwing the broken pieces across the room. Her cries weren't enough to drown out the memory. At no point in the last millennia had they ever been.

She screamed with even greater force this time and ripped at herself. Pain seared through her skull anew, and when she pulled her hand away, it held a clump of hair. Her gaze drifted to her full-length mirror. Her reflection was unrecognizable with dark hair, pale skin, and rage distorting the natural softness in her face. Ever since the ritual, her hair had begun growing out black. It was now all naturally black, but her handmaidens had bleached it blonde for her public appearance. It seemed now that her reflection was truer than she was.

It said:

> "I warned you that I would destroy the light
> in you. Look at you! Hands that held mercy
> are full of blood! I thought you were the key,
> but I am. I unlocked your mind to spite
> and drove your hands to kill the acolyte."

As her reflection crawled toward her, she found herself approaching the mirror. They touched their hands against each others, only the glass separating them, and Labeth saw herself through the reflection's eyes. The world was split. She was split and didn't know where she existed.

> "I do not want the stars that will not see
> me by destroying she who heard my plea.
> Please hear me now and leave me to the night."

They grabbed the mirror and slammed it face down onto the floor. The breaking of the glass sent a spike of pain through their chest. They doubled over on hands and knees, crying out.

> "Your virtue worsens my pain all the time
> as your spirit can't help but reject mine!"

Violent shaking overtook Labeth till she had fully dropped to the floor, unable to move, unable to leave the pain, unable to leave the Jemalgee. On her hands bled small cuts from where she'd pressed them into the glass. She felt certain that there was no other person, nor creature, beside the Jemalgee that deserved to be pitied more than she. It was the final step of unity between her and him—that she would also go mad in this torment caused by her own choices.

As she lay there, the thought she'd been pushing away all year rose to her lips.

> "What have I done? I thought that I could save
> you, but I've only let it swallow us.
> The blood's running way too much, way too much.
> Was hoping in him just a big mistake?"

The next week, they tried to reverse the ritual. Ever since the Mallinor incident, the people had been lining the streets in protest. They didn't want a Jemalgee-possessed crown princess. One death was all it took to make them forget how she had saved their lives.

Labeth understood. Everyone who had warned her had been right. She was fooling with entities far more powerful than she, and she was a boulder on the edge of a cliff threatening to fall. She hadn't wanted to give up. She'd kept that thought locked away, but the Jemalgee knew it as well as she, and he wanted to let her go.

So she, her mother, and the priests returned to the Celestial to release Labeth from her promise. But when the clay-oil mixture was ignited, it didn't transform into glass but lit her arms on fire. Since she'd been chained again, she fell onto her back and writhed, screaming in agony. Cool water washed over her, and the pain stopped devouring her but stayed to simmer on her arms. She dared not look at them but instead trained her eyes on the black sky overhead. How Dior must be laughing at her: *You asked to reap this darkness, and you'll burn by the tortures you've heard.*

In the distance, her mother yelled at the priests. There was supposed to be a spell that would've protected Labeth from the flame if the ritual hadn't worked. It must have been at least partially in place since not all of Labeth's body had burned, just her arms, but whoever had been in charge of the spell would no doubt be stripped of his priesthood and maybe even imprisoned. Labeth couldn't care about that; she was in so much pain.

As someone unchained her and wrapped her arms in damp cloths, she heard her mother yell, "What went wrong?"

Dlanacen responded, "I'm not sure, Your Majesty. We did everything the same as last time. It should've worked unless. . ." He lowered his voice into a stage whisper, "it doesn't want to let go."

His word echoed into her mind. To all others, it would seem the most plausible explanation—a greedy Jemalgee not wanting to let go of a woman as he tortured her to madness—but Labeth knew it wasn't true, so she dug into Dlanacen's soul. For this ritual and the original one, he'd been the main performer; the other priests were mere support. He had changed the words, only slightly so no one without his mystic knowledge would notice, and had guaranteed the ritual would fail. He didn't want to help Labeth because an incapacitated crown princess—especially a difficult one—gave him more power.

A guard tried to pick her up, but she fought out of his grip toward Dlanacen and her mother. "Liar!" she screamed. "You made it fail!"

Her mother and the high priest stared at her horrified as she continued fighting against the guard trying to carry her away. "He doesn't want it! He doesn't want it!" The guard still wouldn't let her go. The Jemalgee was about to rise and strike when the guard pressed a smelly rag to her face. After a few breaths, she fell unconscious.

Reshelia was eating with Asanilph and their mother when a guard interrupted to say that Labeth had been found wandering in the gardens again. Ever since she had joined with *it*—Reshelia refused to call it a he like Labeth—she'd been mostly confined to her room. Labeth consented. But still she would find her way into the gardens, always at night. And no one knew how she sneaked past her guards. Palace servants rumored that the princess escaped into the city to indulge in the debaucheries every Jemalgee chased. They viewed her as less human, said that the princess was gone. Reshelia wondered if she should do the same.

The queen sighed and closed her eyes for a moment. "Did you not increase the sedatives in her meals?"

"Yes, we have," replied the guard. "But she still found a way out. The sedatives must not work on the Jemalgee magic."

Jemalgee magic? Reshelia about rolled her eyes at the new coined term. Before all of this, people would just refer to the powers of a Jemalgee, but now the whole idea of Jemalgee magic had formed like Labeth was a witch who could cast spells with a flick of her wrist like the people in the other sections of Azain. Labeth could shoot columns of black smoke from her body—something no other possessed person could do. She could also sing with its voice and break glass without touching it. It was strange, but something about referring to it as its own magic irked Reshelia.

She wanted her sister back.

"Go fetch her then," said her mother, not veiling her aggravation or disdain. She'd grown sick of this a long time ago. They all had. Labeth was like a bag of sand they were forced to carry through the shallows of the ocean. With each wave it grew heavier.

"We're trying," said the guard. "Several have been injured."

Reshelia threw her napkin onto the table and stood. "I'll talk to her."

"Wait," said her mother.

"Someone has to bring her home," she replied. "I need to talk to her anyway." She ordered the guard to lead the way. She'd lost her appetite and her nursemaid would lay Lilira down. She had to do this.

Outside, the air was humid as it had rained earlier that day. Fog hadn't yet descended, but nothing could make the already unnatural dark night darker. Reshelia hated going outside under the black sky, but she especially hated it at night. She could barely see her hands in front of her face without a lantern. So many things could be hiding around her.

Three small lights floated in the distance. Lanterns of the guards trying to apprehend Labeth. As Reshelia approached, a howl pierced the night, raising the hair on her neck with its terrifying beauty. On one hand, it was a painful cry of a sweet, wounded animal, and on the other, it rang forward to dominate with its grandness, the wounded creature fighting while yowling its death cry.

Reshelia hurried forward into the line of light around the scene. They stood on a garden terrace looking down onto a raised bed of dead flowers. Among them, Labeth lay in her nightgown, gazing terrified into the sky. Her white gown was covered in dirt, and her hair was tangled. It'd been several months since the anniversary of their victory over the Toa, so her black hair had grown back but no one had been brave enough to cut off the bleached ends.

Taking the steps down, Reshelia approached her sister while all the men with swords watched. Shaking Labeth's shoulder gently, she called her name, but her sister continued staring at the sky. In a breathy voice, she sang:

> "I fall up, my hands tight, I'm lost
> in unspace as stars sing white.
> There's no done, there's no be, no went,
> but blood that all has been spent—."

Labeth rolled onto her side to look at Reshelia. Her eyes were black and wide, focused but seeing nothing. She crawled to the edge of the flowerbed and set her bare feet onto the stone walkway. As Reshelia reached for her elbow, Labeth bolted forward, stumbling back and forth between the stone walls of the path. "Go, go!" she screamed.

> "I don't want to know, know, known.
> Behind eyes, they wait, centuries of stares
> ever since my first affair."

Turning to Reshelia, she froze. A piece of skin underneath her right eye pulsed, and even in the dim light, it was hard not to see how gaunt Labeth had become. There were wrinkles around her eyes that a girl her age should not carry. Her gown hung around her like a sack. Approaching slowly, Reshelia gently grabbed both of her arms. "Labeth," she whispered, repeating it over and over till her sister's eyes focused on her and the muscles beneath Reshelia's fingers softened.

Her sister finally seemed to speak to her rather than at her, and she said, "I feel them call in my bones; their teeth clack on ripped out tongues."

Reshelia wanted to pull away, but she steeled herself. The words had a lilting quality to them like all Jemalgee speech did, but they also seemed to come from Labeth herself, rather than the beast inside. Or did they come from both? Were they now so joined that there was no distinction?

Reshelia calmed her thoughts. She was not a philosopher like Labeth had been. Her sister needed to return to her rooms, and Reshelia would make that happen. Wrapping an arm around Labeth's thin shoulders, Reshelia walked her back to her chambers, one guard in front to light the way and the others following—quite distantly—behind.

When they reached Labeth's bedroom, she dismissed them to return to their stations. Her sister had calmed down, so she figured she could take it from there.

"Thanks for coming for me," Labeth said as Reshelia pulled the ruined nightgown over her head. Though Labeth seemed to have returned, her voice remained dreamy, and she only stood there like a doll as Reshelia cleaned her up. They had increased the drugs they gave her ever since the reverse ritual had failed, hoping to make her bedridden. It worked except for the night walks. Due to the drugs, Labeth was often too weak to take care of herself, so maidservants had to do it. They were paid handsomely to overcome their fear of touching the Jemalgee-possessed princess. Labeth must have gotten used to being taken care of.

"No worries," said Reshelia gently. She feared breaking the spell and sending Labeth back into the spiral.

"I can't tell time anymore. I didn't even realize it was winter till I stepped outside, but it feels like it's been a long time since I've seen you." She smiled at her weakly, and Reshelia grabbed a basin of water and a rag to wipe the dirt off her legs, feet, and hands. "How long has it been?"

"It's been a couple months," Reshelia said, trying to appear nonchalant, to hide how much the time away hurt her but also how much she feared her.

"You used to not be away for so long."

Pulling a new nightgown over Labeth's head, Reshelia replied with the common excuse of busyness and led her to sit on the edge of her bed.

"That's not all of it," said Labeth.

Reshelia froze. "Well. . Um. . ." Should she lie? But there was no time, for a cold presence touched her soul. She lurched back. "Stop that!" It didn't matter that the Jemalgee had saved her from her grief. She never wanted to know its touch again. Especially not from her sister. Her thoughts were supposed to be private.

"Mother's making you heir to the throne," said Labeth. She stared at the floor, unmoving for too long.

"I'm sorry." Reshelia took one step forward. "But it has to be this way."

It was a long time before Labeth spoke again:

> "'A fake that all can see,' my bird said. 'You
> will rot among the living dead and prove
> that there is nothing you can do.'"

"Shh, don't say that," said Reshelia, meaning to comfort her, but when she stepped close, Labeth grabbed her arms and shook her.

> "I opened the door 'cause of the whispers inside,
> and no such sound can slice thoughts like it.
> I hold the beginning—ginning—dinging
> with not the other, and the whispers continue.
> They come inside to inscribe their sins and names."

Her words were rushed, and tears began to stream down her cheeks. Repeating senseless words of comfort, Reshelia lightly but firmly pushed her sister back onto the bed. She cradled her body as Labeth lay down, saying, "I don't want to hear them. I want to go home. Please, take me home. Just take me home."

Holding back her own tears, Reshelia hurried out of the room. Labeth was worst than lost. She was Unfound, a rotted shell of her nature. There was nothing that could be done, so

Reshelia walked away. It would be the last time she saw her sister.
Alive.

Jemalgee

I'm sorry, but you weren't you anymore after that incident with your sister. They drugged you so much that you were barely there, only a shivering form in the base of your consciousness. I would've tried to comfort you, but my rage tormented you more. I know what it is like to suffer for eternity, so I couldn't let you stay that way. I would've wanted someone to do the same to me (if it were possible).

There were many ways I could've taken your life—a precise slit from the glass of a window, a rope made of bedsheets. But I wanted to give you one last piece of beauty, so I led you through the woods to your favorite writing spot. Where we met.

We stood on the edge of the cliff one last time, and you looked out at everything. If not for my presence, you wouldn't have been able to see anything beneath Dior's darkness, so there's that at least. The crickets chirped, and the autumn air was cold but fresh. The only thing missing were the stars we both loved and their reflection on the water.

If I could erase one mistake I have made, it would be joining with you.

We stepped off the cliff, and I did not catch you in my smoke this time. Your body broke with a crack, and the death from such a height was instant. As you drifted to the floor, I rose, breaking free of the water and into the sky. You were free of my torment,

and I intended to flee as far away from any human as I could—
even to the Unfound World if I must.

But as I turned away from your home, a force I couldn't win
against pulled me back to the palace. Even with you free, the ritual wouldn't let me go. It dragged me in through cracks in the
palace walls and into your sister Reshelia. I knew instantly that
we would be bound in the same way. She woke and screamed as
you had when we slaughtered those soldiers.

I should've guessed it. I will continue. I always continue,
damned and damning others.

READ ON

for

EXCLUSIVE
BONUS MATERIAL

Azain: A World of Worlds + Map

The Mystic Codex

**Sneak Peek of The One and the Other
Volume Two**

The Known World

Map of Azain

c. 1243

From *Azain:*
A World of Worlds

In 0 A.S. (After Separation), an unexplained force created magical boundaries that divided our world of Azain into eleven sections, each obeying their own magical rules. When one crosses the boundary into another section, they no longer obey the rules of their original one, but of the new.

The sections can be divided into three main categories:

1. Magic Sections
2. Species Sections
3. Other

Our section Loreiak is a magic section with special, additional properties. Each magic section has its own unique magic and ours is channeling magic. The existence of the Duals and our connection to the Unfound World also make our section unique. Since channeling magic and the Duals are so intertwined, it is theorized that they could not be separated, and that's why they both appear in our section. If a mystic were to travel into another section, they would no longer be able to use channeling magic to cast any sort of ritual.

This is true for any other type of magic. Given our isolated position—we are the only section completely surrounded by water—we know very little of the other sections. There exists flesh and bone magic, and there are rumors of others but we cannot be sure.

Another type of section are the Species Sections. There is only one, and some books will lump this in with the Other category, claiming there are only magic and non-magic sections. Books from the before age speak to there being more species than just human and liasu, and since there is so much of the world we Lo-reiakians are ignorant of, we cannot be sure. The liasu exist to the west across the sea. They are stronger and faster than the average human, and many have abilities such as moving objects without touching them, climbing walls like spiders, or clairvoyance and many more. Their power comes from a dark liquid found in the buds of flowers that grow in their section. They drink it, calling it Earth's blood.

Finally are the sections that fit into neither category. The main one is that of our neighbors. No magic can exist within their boundaries, but their people have an affinity for technology that surpasses any other section. While some of their technology can be traded across our boundary and still work, it is not known if this is true for all. The main countries in the section are Toa, Agiede, and Saka, though there are more smaller ones. Toa on the western coast is the closest to us, and the city of Tet-quan can be reached easily by boat.

They are our only trading partners because of our isolation by sea. Any goods we receive from the other sections come through their ports. Their ships are some of the only ones to brave the open sea to trade with the liasu and survive. After some point, as one travels away from all land, all magic ceases to work. And in the open sea are dangerous monsters, such as sea dragons, that can sink a ship within minutes, leaving no survivors.

It is because of these barriers that Loreiakians keep mostly to themselves. We have the food, water, and resources that we need for our thriving little section. Ever since the time of the Unifying Wars, we have not needed to fight. Channeling magic, our gift, does not give itself to fighting like some of the other magics, and many have taken this as a sign that we are to be a peaceful people.

The Mystic Codex

written in 1134 A.S.
by High Priest Uphalinik

The truth of the saying *"every one thing is also another"* is not merely a proverb but is the blood that runs through Loreiak's veins. Every one thing is also another—that which is mundane and that which is supernatural. Our world is layered as the worlds are layered. It creates the unique beauty of our country, of its people, and of mysticism itself that the other sections of Azain do not know of. It is believed that when crossing the magical borders, even the structures that form our bodies would change, losing this layeredness, though very little has been done to study it.

But I digress. If you are reading this, welcome new acolyte. I will no longer overwhelm you with the philosophical machinations of mysticism—those are for later instruction—but instead start from the beginning with the foundations of our practice.

What exactly is mysticism?

Mysticism is a system of practices and beliefs centered around channeling magic, the eleven Duals, and Loreiak's unique connection to the In-Between, the Unfound World, and the creatures of both.

Let's begin with channeling magic.

Channeling Magic

There are many different systems of magic that exist in Azain: Bone, Flesh, and Dream magic are the ones we know of, though it is suspected there are more littered through the sections. [If you are not yet familiar with the properties of the magical boundaries that divide Azain into its sections, I suggest familiarizing yourself with material from *Azain: A World of Worlds* before continuing further.] Before the Separation in 0 A.S., all magics existed together in chaos and were separated, one given to each Magic Section, by the unknown force that created the boundaries. This allows them to be used by the practitioners of its section without interacting with the others in spontaneous and grave ways. Loreiak—our section—was blessed with channeling magic.

Channeling magic allows one to either channel his or her consciousness or energy into something else, or to channel some other energy into oneself. The way one harnesses channeling magic is through rituals. Rituals are a combination of materials and poetry. The poetry often has a structure that has to be filled in by the practitioner rather than set words. While it is possible to harness channeling magic without the materials or poetry, it is very dangerous and unpredictable. The materials and the words of the poetry are duals that help us guide the magic [see Chapter 3].

A practitioner's power is limited by what rituals they know or have access to, so it is very important that you study *The 100 Most Common Rituals*. A copy of the tome sits on a pedestal in the Eastern Library. You may stand and study it during daylight hours and with the supervision of a priest to turn the pages for you. You are not allowed to touch it to prevent smearing or damaging the tome.

I will briefly go over the main types of rituals.

Possession

Possession is the most well-known, albeit infamous, form of channeling magic. It includes channeling another entity into your mind or channeling your consciousness into another entity. These entities can be human, animal, ghost, Jemalgee, or creatures of the Unfound World, such as sleep demons and the dybbuk, or even abstractions, like emotions and memories.

The common people have mediums who make money by channeling the dead spirit of another's loved one into their consciousness, so they can speak with them. Many are frauds. Here in the priesthood of Loreiak, we understand the dangers of interacting with anything from the Unfound World, and conversing with the dead, especially for financial gain, is strictly forbidden.

Every acolyte will learn possession involving animals, emotions, and memories. The other types are reserved for only the highest of the priests. It takes a strong will to not be overcome by the possessor and lose oneself in the process. However, every acolyte will be taught one ritual for human possession, though it is only to be used in the most dire of circumstances. There will be consequences if it is not so. This is not because we are worried about people being taken advantaged of—you must have the other's consent to possess them—but the act of possession can cause both entities to turn mad if done without a delicate, trained hand.

Animals, however, are not sentient enough. You do not need their consent, and they are much easier to possess. Only the Jemalgee and some of the other creatures of the Unfound World have the power to possess a human without their consent.

Internal Channeling

A subcategory of possession is Internal Channeling. It is when the channel and the entity being channeled are of the same, usually a person. Some rituals can affect a person's perception of his/herself, can hide memories, can disguise pain, etc. A talisman or potion must be used if the practitioner is performing the ritual on his or herself but is unnecessary if someone else is performing the ritual.

Dual Channeling

Dual Channeling involves channeling one of the Duals (such as light, darkness, mind, blood, wind) into an object for a particular use.

The most common reason is for communication. Every priest at the end of their acolyte training will be gifted a circular mirror for communication purposes. By then, you will know how to channel your consciousness into the mirror of another's, so you may speak with them without having to be in the same room. It is not necessary to use your own mirror to call another as you will learn. The mirror is only for receiving calls. However, most priests prefer it if the receiver also channels their consciousness into the sender's mirror so both parties may be seen. By mirror is not the only way to communicate, though it is the most common. Other objects include sheets, fabric, and liquids.

The next most common type of Dual Channeling is healing. One can channel their life force into another to speed up the healing process of their body. This is done mostly through small blood sacrifices that do not take the life of the giver or blood gifts. Unless the wound is minor, the healing process cannot happen immediately. It is more to heal a person in a few days when it would normally take weeks, and a week or two when they would usually take months.

Finally, talismans and potions are common ways people can use channeling magic to affect others or even themselves. They can channel their grief into a talisman or erase it by drinking a potion. They can also influence another's emotions or mind by getting them to wear or use the talisman or drink the potion. Even in the dark of the night, light can be channeled into an object to use like a lantern. There are many other similar rituals that will be covered in Chapter 5.

The Eleven Duals

Now that we have covered the basics of channeling magic, we can talk about the eleven Duals. Remember: every one thing is also another, and we have found eleven such correlations, called duals, that act as the foundation for the structure of our world and our practice. I will now go through each of them in the order of their appearance in the calendar.

Blood is Life

A person's life force is their blood. When one loses blood or their blood slows, they are losing their life force, which is why they die or become weak. A blood gift is accompanied by a special ritual to transfer the life force of one person to another.

Not only is blood the dual to life, but it is also connected to the strength and power of an entity. It is why at the beginning of every year, a person voluntarily sacrifices themselves to bring good fortune to the new year. It is also important everyone provides their monthly sacrifices of goats, foxes, chickens, etc to contribute to the strength of Loreiak. If we do not, there could be grave consequences. The Unfound World beneath us growls and the ghustaugness always desires more, so we must sacrifice to add strength to Loreiak and stave off the Darkness.

Throughout the year, the common folk bring more sacrifices for various things—good health, a prayer for fortune, a plentiful harvest, or increase a ritual's strength. Performing the actual sacrificing is the main duty of a priest. You will learn more about the proper ways to skin and flay an animal for sacrifice in Chapter 8 before moving on to the practical application. Until then, new acolytes are responsible for cleaning the temples through the day.

Light is **Purity**

Different forms of light have different levels of purity. The word for the purest light is lenou, the antithesis of the ghustaugness, the Ultimate Darkness. Lightning is also one of the purest forms of light on this earth. The Jemalgee who have not fallen exist as the stars above us, composed of the purest light. The fallen ones, however, are composed only of ghustaugness. They can be either or, not both. However, humans have equal capacity for good and evil. We carry different levels of both throughout our lives. Children are born with the most purity they will ever have, and as they age, the Ghustaugness grows inside of them as it does with all things. It is up to the person to determine how much of themselves the Ghustaugness devours.

Plants are **Time**

Plants are the dual of time—their first growths are the start of something, their continual growth shows the passage of time, and their death shows the end of a period. This truth is shown through all nature: tree rings keep track of the years; Leedathou flowers open in the day and close at night, mirroring the cycle of days; plants die in the fall, but not before dispersing their seed for new plants to grow in the spring. This mirrors the passing of one year into another. This is why at celebrations for something new like a marriage, a new year, a birth, a plant will often be gifted to the celebrators.

Fluids are **Emotions**

All bodily fluids, except for blood, are Duals to emotions. All these fluids exist in harmony in a person, but the intensifying of an emotion leads to the increased production of the corresponding bodily fluid. Expelling the fluid helps one to overcome or process the emotion. A person who becomes sick is filled with phlegm and can only regain their energy when the phlegm has passed through the system. However, consuming the bodily fluid can also increase that emotion as in the case of consuming sexual bodily fluids will only increase that person's lust.

Tears	=	Sadness
Semen/Lubricant	=	Lust
Bile	=	Anger/Unhappiness
Phlegm	=	Lethargy
Water	=	Serenity/Happiness
Saliva	=	Hunger
Feces	=	Disgust
Sweat	=	Fear

Energy is **Knowledge**

One must expend energy to gain or use knowledge, so knowledge is the Dual to energy. When one gains knowledge, they gain strings of energy that forever exist inside them until old age when they begin to lose them. That is why the deterioration of the mind is quickly followed by the weakening of the body. It is important for the body to have fuel in order to learn and know things, so all priests are expected to maintain a healthy diet.

Words are Power

Words change the world. They call forth and control people, construct laws, and reveal and shape beliefs wherever they are heard. They can help one person exert power over another or free people from their chains. This is why rituals require a poem because it is on words that the power of channeling magic is carried.

Mirrors reveal Thoughts

Mirrors or glass and other reflective objects are special channels where one can view into their own mind or soul. We can use rituals to reveal things that the person might not have been able to discern otherwise. It is easiest to channel one's thoughts or words through glass—though there are other things that may act as channels. Several witnesses who have found themselves in the In-Between recall a maze of mirrors showing their past and innermost thoughts.

Earth is Barrier

Earth is barriers or boundaries. That's why in rituals, the practitioners surround themselves with some type of earth (commonly chalk, sand, or paint). This is to keep the power of the ritual inside the boundaries so the practitioner can more easily draw on it. Different types of earth produce boundaries of varying strengths with obsidian dust providing the strongest that we know of at this time. Earth is also a way to bind oneself to another thing or person. Painting oneself with the same earth will bind the practitioners of a ritual and their power.

Smoke is Spirit

Spirits of the dead or of supernatural creatures often take the form of smoke. Mediums breathe in this smoke when they call forth ghosts from the Unfound World. And this correlation between smoke and spirit is also why the Jemalgee appear like smoke when they are not in their true form.

Darkness is Ghustaugness

The ghustaugness is the ultimate darkness that seeks to destroy all light and the earth with it. It surrounds every star and is in every shadow. It runs through all of our world, though it is strongest in the furthest regions of the Unfound one where it is believed to have originated. It is the most corrupt nature of people and Jemalgee. As priests, some of our work involves interacting with the Ghustaugness, so remember to be on your guard so as to not be consumed by it. Do not let yourselves become enslaved to it like the fallen Jemalgee. They are so enslaved that they are it. Ghustaugness is the darkness that surrounds every star and is in every shadow.

Wind is **Nothing**

It is not so much that the wind or breath is the entity of nothing, but that the movement of wind or breath sweeps what is something away into nothing. A person's breath blows out a candle. The winds sweep away life. The movements of the sun, moon, and stars sweep the days and years into the past where they exist as nothing. A person's last breath carries their spirit away.

Special Mystics

Every Loreiakian has the power to practice mysticism. As the priesthood, we have been set apart to specialize in its practice. We protect our country, ensure its prosperity through sacrifice, and serve its people. There are others who have been set apart from birth for specific purposes by the universe itself. When discovered, they are encouraged to join our ranks.

Iriduns

The first and most rare are iriduns. They are the only entity in Loreiak with the ability to open portals between the Found and Unfound Worlds. Not even the Jemalgee have this power. Also, their bodies can act as channels for the conducting of knowledge from the Unfound World into tattoos that temporarily appear on their bodies. This phenomenon is still largely unexplained—one of the beautiful mysteries of these complex worlds we live with.

Bloodgivers

Next are bloodgivers who are able to give blood and their life force energy to anyone. Not everyone's life force will harmonize with another, but the blood of these givers works with everyone's.

Star Seers

Lastly are the Star Seers. Foretelling through the stars is not an ability blessed at birth, but one that involves decades of hard study to develop any sort of proficiency before you can reliably read the sky. What will be covered in Chapter 10 is but a small fraction of the theoretical knowledge involved.

The Realms

There are three layers of worlds existing like floors of a building. On the top is ours, the Found World, and on the bottom is the Unfound World. The In-Between as you can guess acquires its namesake from its placement. As you are already no doubt familiar with the Found World, we will begin with the Unfound.

The Unfound World

The Unfound World is a realm that exists below not only Loreiak but the whole known universe. Like a coral reef, some parts of the Unfound World stretch closer to the surface of our world, while others are hidden further away in its depths. Loreiak has a special connection to this other world because our country is placed where the Unfound reaches closest to ours.

Not much is known about the Unfound World—it is not recommended that one journey far into it. It is massive, seemingly infinite, and full of dangerous beings, some of which are able to slip through into our world. We will cover the creatures that we know of next.

Known Creatures of the Unfound World

THE DYBBUK are the dislocated souls of someone who has been deceased and trapped in the Unfound World for a long time. They appear as either mist or smoke and can only slip into our world while in this form. Once here, they take over a host body to complete any unfinished business they have from their life. Most have been dead for centuries before they devolve into one of the Dybbuk, so there is rarely anything remaining of their previous life. They are mad creatures and will exact what revenge they see fit on anyone they choose.

THE GASHAD are gigantic skeletons formed by the amassed bones of people who died of starvation. Unlike the Dybbuk, they are mindless, without ambition. They wander on lonely roads and bite off the heads of travelers and drink the spraying blood.

WENDIGOS are malevolent and cannibalistic creatures with the heads of animals such as deer, wolves, or birds but the bodies of humans. They can exist on their own and devour people, but they can also possess a person, infecting them with desires for human flesh. They are never satisfied and constantly search for new victims.

THE WORLD WALKERS are closer to myth than reality. One's appearance is that of a horse made with white light with a single horn protruding from its forehead. They glow even among the densest ghustaugness, and it is believed that if you capture one and drink it, you will become immortal. They travel between all worlds, found and unfound, but none have been seen in recent history. All accounts made in present day have been disproved, and it is widely accepted that World Walkers are mere myths.

THE FALLEN JEMALGEE are the ones of their kinds who chose to leave their place in the sky as stars to meddle with the affairs of earth for pleasure, power, wealth, etc. Since Jemalgee only have the capacity to be either purely light or purely darkness, once they tasted the sins of what they craved, they were forever corrupted by the ghustaugness. They were exiled from the sky, damned to roam the earth where they wreak havoc on anything in their path.

They are creatures of such humongous size that they are in-conceivable to the human eyes. They are as large as mountains and roam the earth in smoke-like clouds since their bodies are too big to exist comfortably in our world. All accounts of their true forms come from people who have seen them in the In-Be-tween while they were possessed. The Jemalgee appear in a much smaller version of their true form there. The corrupted ones are all dark colors that appear as black to most eyes, though in their pure state they glow as bright colors. The Jemalgee have a long body like a snake but with four clawed feet. They have a long neck and a skull like a scaled horse with spikes in place of a mane that run all the way to its tail. Its skin and three sets of wings are leathery like that of a bat.

Another unique fact about the Jemalgee is that they speak only in poetry. Different Jemalgee have been known to prefer different styles and poetic devices. They have the most beautiful voices, beyond anything a human could hope to produce. They are neither male nor female in nature, though the voice may seem as more female when coming from a female host or male when coming from a male host. We also tend to perceive a gendered voice from the Jemalgee in their smoke form, depending on one's preferences. With their voices and poetry, they craft songs through which they read people's souls, speaking any person's most intimate desires, fears, traits, and flaws into the air so they must face them. They may be relieved or horrified by what they hear. It is a tactic many Jemalgee use to overwhelm their victims by the darkest parts of their own natures.

The Jemalgee spend their immortal years roaming Loreiak, possessing human hosts whenever they please to pursue pleasure or violence—whichever satisfies their fancy that day. The magical borders separating Loreiak from the rest of Azain are one of the only things known to contain them. For an unknown reason, they cannot exist beyond Loreiak. Uncomfortable with the confinement, many have retreated or been banished to the Unfound

World where they can indulge their dark desires on a grander scale. Most priests never face a Jemalgee, but it is something they are called to protect our people from. In addition to their power over one's mind, they retain their strength and power of their true form even in their smoke one. They can tear multiple men limb from limb at once and destroy whole cities and make mountains tremble. It is important to prepare yourself and exercise the appropriate caution. Never face one alone (See Chapter 9 for methods).

The In-Between

Between the Found and Unfound Worlds lies the aptly named realm of the In-Between. It is a place that can only be visited within one's dreams. Everyone sees something different (places and people from their lives or ones they have never seen before), but one place that many people have visited is the Maze of Mirrors.

Remember that the Dual of Thoughts and the Mind are mirrors and other reflective surfaces. Some believe that the In-Between is the mind and that its purpose is to show us what we don't want to face. Others believe that it is the realm of the Sandman. His silhouette appears human but his body is entirely made of sand. By sprinkling sand on a person's eyelids, he creates a barrier that traps them in their dreams until he releases them. During this, he walks into their minds and drags them down into the In-Between or the Unfound World. Creatures called Sleep Demons are at his beck and call. They seize any dreamers, raping and paralyzing them so even if the people wake, they cannot move until the demon is finished.

Much remains unknown about the In-Between. It is difficult to decipher fact from myth especially for those who have never been.

Conclusion

This concludes chapter one of the Mystic Codex. You learned the basics of mysticism, such as channeling magic, the Duals, and the three planes of existence: Found, Unfound, and In-Between. The following chapters will cover these topics in more depth and be paired with practicals for casting rituals.

EXCLUSIVE SNEAK PEEK

of

THE ONE AND THE OTHER
VOLUME TWO

NOTE TO THE READER:

If you've read *The One-Sided Coin*, I'm sorry for leaving you on the cliffhanger that I did. I thought I would be more finished with Volume Two by now, but *The Damned Ones* went from what was supposed to be a flashback sequence in *The One-Sided Coin* to a full-length novel.

Thank you for your patience. Here is a sneak peek of Volume Two as a token of my gratitude. Be aware that this is a first draft. There may be significant changes between this and what occurs in the final version. I am very happy with the chapter though and am excited to share it with you.

I

As they watched the white beacon flare into the sky, Monoria fainted. Attalayla heard a thud and felt the space beside her empty. It felt far off, for she was so enraptured—terrified—by the beacon. Waking to her senses, she turned and saw Monoria unconscious on the ground. She knelt down and pressed her hands onto the other girl's stomach. It was covered in blood from where Eshrusk had shot her. It was a lot. Too much.

Then, the beacon shut off, taking all of its light with it. Attalayla couldn't see anything under the starless and moonless sky. The sky of Loreiak had been covered by something dark a couple hundred years ago, so only the barest scrap of sunlight, moonlight, and starlight filtered through. It was nearly impossible to see anything at night. Monoria somehow could, probably because of her connection to what she called her Ghost—a Jemalgee which was a being as corrupt as it was powerful. Without Monoria's guidance, Attalayla was near blind. Her only source of light at the moment were the headlights of the Lightning Strike, a machine that could fly into the air and shoot a blast worthy of its name.

And it was hunting them.

Lightning was the only thing that could kill the Jemalgee inside Monoria, and would surely kill her and Attalayla as well. They'd already shot it once at the Celestial, obliterating the mystic monument. They'd run from it the first time, but Attalayla was scared that would be the last time. They needed to get out of its light.

It circled around the ruins of the Celestial, searching. They had some time at least. But Monoria was bleeding out quickly.

Attalayla went to the remains of the car. The lightning blast had flipped it onto its side and thrown the supplies from its trunk everywhere. She found the medical kit in a duffel bag and returned to bandage Monoria. Fortunately, the bullet had gone out the other side, so all she had to do was stop the bleeding and dress the wound. She pressed gauze against Monoria's side, and soon her hands and clothes were bloody. The warm, sticky liquid clung to her skin. It was so hard to see in the near darkness. But she felt the spikiness of the rat's coat, heard it squeal as she ripped into it with her mouth, her teeth mashing on its guts. She spit, crying out and falling onto her back.

Above her were bare tree branches and not the dilapidated buildings of her hometown Ilion. There was no rat. Not anymore. It had all been a memory. Breathing deeply, she dug her fingers into the dirt beneath her to remind her of where she really was. She willed herself to get back to the present, to fight the parts of her mind seeking to drive her insane. She wouldn't let that happen.

Sitting up again, she finished dressing Monoria's wounds. The lightning strike was still circling the Celestial and hadn't found them yet, but they needed to seek cover. Attalayla grabbed under Monoria's armpits and pulled her into the trees. Monoria was heavier than Attalayla thought she would be, or perhaps Attalayla was really that weak. During her time in the KDCC and off the streets, she had grown soft and weak with no need to survive and forage for food like she'd had to in the slums. She had remained determined though, and that's what fueled her to go on.

Not far behind the treeline was a stone building. Vines and tree roots pierced into its walls. She pulled Monoria into it and fell back onto the concrete floor, exhausted. How were they going to get out of this? Attalayla didn't know if dressing the wound would do very much, and there was no telling if Monoria would survive with all the blood loss. Her falling unconscious wasn't a good sign, and there was no one to help them. They were on their own, a situation Attalayla was used to, but things had never been quite so dire as this. They needed to get through the night. They needed to hide from the Lightning Strike. That was what she chose to focus on.

She tried to shake Monoria awake, but there was no response. Attalayla held her ear over Monoria's mouth to check that she still breathed. She did.

She could abandon her, Attalayla thought. She couldn't carry her, and she was what the secularists wanted anyway. She could run, grab some supplies left in the car, and try to get through the mountains back to the cabin they had stayed in the night before. It was her only chance of survival. Attalayla pushed the thought away. No, she wouldn't abandon Monoria to die, not after all that she had done for her and what she had told her in the city Ithli. *I see flashes of what a life where I'm happy could be like. And it's with you. I need you to come with me. You're all I have left.* Monoria hadn't abandoned her, so neither would she. She would fight till they got out of this mess or till one or both of them died.

She dug through the rest of the duffel bag that had housed the medical pack. There was some rope, only a few feet, a bottle of water, and a pair of strange goggles. When Attalayla tried them on, she could see, though everything was a weird shade of green. Night vision goggles. And from the medical pack, she grabbed the pair of scissors. They were more suited for cutting bandages, but they would do if the time came.

Wearing the goggles, she peered outside at the Lightning Strike. She didn't know why it didn't just torch the whole place, unless the machine had to recharge in between blasts. How long would they have? Two small beads of light fell from the bottom of the Lightning Strike, gliding down to the earth. They were people using parachutes. They were sending out a ground team to search for them. They would be armed. Once they found the overturned car, finding Attalayla and Monoria would be easy, and Attalayla didn't have the strength to carry Monoria any farther. She tightened her grip on the scissors. She would have to fight.

Celond felt guilty leaving to take a shower, but he needed to cleanse himself of the filth of that day. All its violence and frustrations clung to him like wet snow. Things had settled down. The patients had completely subdued the KDCC, imprisoning the nurses and doctors in the underground tunnels. Things were almost calm, so Celond had the chance to step away. A lot of the patients were exhausted from fighting.

As the water streamed down his back, Celond thought of Attalayla. They'd searched the entire compound for her, and she was nowhere to be found. Karack had said that she was no longer in the KDCC but had been taken with Eshrusk and Monoria to wherever they were going to heal Monoria of the parasite. He had laughed. She should already be dead, he'd said when Celond had demanded why.

No. She couldn't be dead. But what if she was?

Celond started to sob as his guilt and frustration weighed on him. He should never have left Attalayla in the KDCC to return to Regemir with his mother. He had doomed her to be tortured and possibly killed at the hands of the secularists. Would he ever see her again? It was all his fault.

He punched the tile wall of the shower. Again and again. His knuckles were already cracked a little from punching Karack, and punching the wall further opened them until they bled. He watched the blood flow over his fingers and down into the drain. Before the last week he had rarely lashed out in anger and never violently. He didn't know himself anymore. He remembered holding the knife to Karack's throat and trying to strangle him in the prison. What was he becoming?

He exited the shower and pressed some toilet paper to his knuckles to stop the bleeding, and then dressed into some clothes he had stolen from the KDCC supplies. He couldn't put on his old ones with the blood stains. Leaning against the wall, he rubbed his eyes. He wanted to stop thinking. He was so tired, but he couldn't go to sleep. He had some things he needed to do.

He went to the hospital wing where Rosollin had been taken after being shot. He hadn't checked on him since everything that had happened. He might be dead. Celond's chest grew tight as he turned the corner into the hospital wing. If he was dead, it would be Celond's fault. There were multiple people in the hospital wing getting their wounds treated from the fighting. More than just Rosollin had been shot. In one of the hallways was a gurney with a white sheet over the body of someone who had died. Celond turned away and peeked into the hospital rooms until he found the one with Rosollin. He was alive but sleeping. Phania sat by his side. She smiled when Celond entered.

"How is he?" he asked

"A nurse says that he's stable."

"The nurses are helping us?"

"They don't really have a choice. We're holding them hostage."

The admittance was like another punch to Celond's gut. That hadn't been something he had intended, but the nurses had been complicit in imprisoning people, telling them that they were insane, and doing who knows what else to them. How many more people had they striven to drive insane? There had been torture devices in the underground tunnels and people locked in cells.

Taking over the KDCC was what had to be done to save everyone.

Celond touched Rosollin's shoulder and gave it a little squeeze.

"Thank you," said Phania.

He drew back. "What?"

"Thank you," she repeated, "for helping us fight for our freedom. I can go home and see my family now because of you."

Celond just nodded. He couldn't bring himself to say you're welcome or take credit for the chaos he had incited. They weren't out of the woods yet.

Burrou rushed in, out of breath. "We have a situation."

He led Celond outside as he explained what was going on. There were six cars inside the mental institution's garage, and when Burrou and a few other patients went to check them out, they found a group of patients stealing one of them. They tried to stop them, saying that they were going to make decisions about how to use the cars as a group. When the thieves wouldn't listen, a fight broke out and they were able to leave with the van. They drove so fast out of the compound they broke through the KDCC's gates.

Inside the garage were the remaining five cars and a group of patients, many of whom were armed with guns and tasers. One man lay on the ground, his head in another's arms. Celond rushed to go to him, scared he had been shot, but the man holding him said he had just been tased and was recovering. It still made Celond sick. "Why did they do this?" he asked.

"They want out," said Burrou simply. "People have been antsy to get out of this hellhole for months, and now some of them are treating it like it's a free for all."

"More will leave once it becomes light again," said a woman. "It's too dark to travel on foot now, though some might try to steal the cars again."

"We should lock the garage up," said Burrou. "We'll need all these cars to help us escape."

Escape, thought Celond. That was the next step. How were they going to do that?

"Burrou's right," he said. "If people want to leave, they can leave on foot, but we need these cars if we're to get as many people out of here as soon as possible."

They locked the garage up, and when they were done, Burrou gave Celond the key. Celond looked at it for a bit at first, not sure if he should take it. "I thought it would be best if you held onto it," Burrou said.

Relenting, Celond took it. As they walked away, Burrou asked what their next move should be.

"To be honest, I don't know," replied Celond. "Let's just get through the night. We'll decide in the morning." Celond walked away and headed back to the main building. He wanted so badly to go to sleep, but he couldn't. His mind wouldn't rest, and his feet took him to Karack's office. Maybe there was information there about Attalayla or something else that could help them.

Karack's office was dark except for the light of the TVs showing the camera feed from all around the KDCC. Sitting in a wingback chair, watching with a bottle of gin dangling between his fingers was Jeriph. Celond turned on the light. Groaning, Jeriph took another sip of his gin. "What are you doing here?"

"I came to see if there's anything we could use." Celond headed over to Karack's desk and flipped through the papers on top. "What are you doing here?"

"Trying to get some peace and quiet." He glared at Celond, letting the other man fill in his true meaning. Celond didn't care. He'd been through too much that night. Sitting in Karack's chair, he searched the drawers.

"I saw what went down with the cars," Jeriph said. "I don't understand. Why lock it up? Just let everyone leave. We freed them. You got to be a hero for someone at least." That barb stung Celond but he focused on his search.

"We need those cars to try to get the maximum number of people out of here." Celond replied.

"Don't you think we've done enough?"

"No." Celond had more to say but stopped when he saw a file with his name on it. He pulled it out and opened it on the desk. Inside were several drawings of star charts. They were all very familiar to him. He had poured over these star charts and constellations for hours back before his days in the KDCC—when he had used a telescope with a special lens to study what was beneath the black sky. It was what he had been imprisoned for. They had said he was insane for studying the sky and seeing something where there was nothing. But many of the KDCC patients had been imprisoned there in order to keep information they had from getting out. Celond still didn't understand why the secularists thought it so necessary to hide the existence of the stars behind the sky.

How did the KDCC have these? At first he thought that these must be the originals he had penned and that the police who had arrested him had given them to Karack as evidence, but he realized that this was not the paper he used to draw on. These were not his drawings, but they were in his handwriting, from his memories.

He flipped through the rest of the star charts, coming to the last page which read: patient put under hypnosis by Dr. Leskin and given the order to draw the star charts from his memory. Afterward memory wiped. There was another note further down: placed strong desire in patient's mind to not escape because he believes that he will be released.

Celond dropped the file in shock, and the rustle of pages caught Jeriph's attention. He sauntered over and looked over Celond's shoulder at the file. "What are you looking at?"

"They hypnotized me."

"Honestly, I'm not surprised." Jeriph took another sip of his gin.

"They made me believe that I would be released, so I wouldn't want to escape with Attalayla." Everything he had been so sure of had been lies and another part of Karack's games. This was more proof that Attalayla had been right about Karack turning him against her. Karack had used him to drive Attalayla insane, and Celond had played right along with him.

"What did they make you do under hypnosis, bark like a dog?" Jeriph chuckled.

Celond handed him a star chart. "They made me draw these."

Jeriph quirked his mouth as he squinted at them. "Interesting." He threw the star charts back onto the desk, obviously uninterested. "Good thing they didn't make you do anything else. I'd hate having them in my brain."

As Jeriph returned to his chair, the phone on Karack's desk started ringing. They both froze, but it kept ringing.

"Are you gonna get that?" asked Jeriph, trying to be nonchalant, but Celond noticed the tenseness that had not been there a few moments before. Celond didn't reply. His heart was in his throat.

Eventually, the phone stopped ringing, and it went to voicemail. A man spoke, "Ionio, this is urgent. You must come to the capital immediately. That beacon means nothing good. Something must've gone wrong with the ritual. Call me back as soon as you get this." The speaker hung up, and neither Celond nor Jeriph spoke for several moments.

"Sorry," said Jeriph, "but Karack can't come to the phone right now."

Celond gave him in an exasperated look. No, he couldn't. And sooner rather than later, the person on the other end of that call would figure out that something was not right at the KDCC.

Monoria couldn't breathe. Water encased her on all sides, and she didn't know which way was up. She pushed and kicked but never seemed to go anywhere. It was hard to move. When she breached the surface, gasping for air, a metallic taste flooded her mouth, and she spit and coughed. She tried to wipe the water from her eyes, but it further rubbed it in, burning them and blurring her vision.

She could barely see the tiniest of lights ahead of her. She struggled toward it till her feet found purchase, and she hauled herself out, collapsing on the shore. The ground was fine black sand. Above her, there was no sky, not even the black one of Loreiak for that at least filtered in a little sunlight and moonlight. It seemed like she was in an underground cave except she could not see the ceiling. There was just nothing.

She felt sticky, discombobulated, and nauseous. When she regained her breath, she crawled toward the light. It was one lone candle in a rusted lantern box. Once she reached its small circle of light, she could see why the water on her felt especially sticky. It wasn't water, but blood. Every last drop of it. In her hair, on her face, soaked into her clothes. She retched, some blood coming out of her lungs as well.

She glanced behind her at the lake she had crawled from, but it was so dark she still couldn't tell that it was blood and not water. She didn't have her night vision here. She saw things as a regular person did before she had become joined with her Ghost.

"What's going on?" she asked him, but there was no answer. She felt different, like something was missing. Had she forgotten something? Or lost something? Why was she here and what had happened? Everything outside the present moment seemed so blurry. She was exhausted and still breathing heavy as if she had done much more than crawl out of a lake. Her limbs shook with weakness. Placing her hand on the lantern's top, she leaned her head against it, drinking in the warmth.

Something barked ahead of her, and she jumped to attention. Out of the darkness came a medium-sized dog with golden brown fur and triangular ears that pointed to the sky. It lunged at her, and Monoria screamed as she fell backward to get away. The dog licked her face and hands when she tried to push it away. She shoved it off, and it whimpered.

Sitting up, she finally got a good look at it. It stared at her with round brown eyes, and she immediately knew that it meant her no harm. After a moment, it approached again, licking her fingers. She offered both hands to let it clean off the blood from them.

As they got more comfortable with each other, her hands found its neck, and it settled into her lap. She stroked its hair, the motion calming her. She felt the rise and fall of its body as it breathed, and she didn't feel so alone or afraid. Though she could not remember much of her life, she knew that it had been a long time since she'd felt the body of another living thing against her.

Leaning over, she rested her head on its back. She didn't know what was going on, but at that moment, she was content and didn't care.

ACKNOWLEDGEMENTS

Another book down. Wow. It's surreal. Ever since *The One-Sided Coin's* release, people have been asking me how I managed to write a book, and I honestly don't know. I am always surprised when I look back at how vast this world of Loreiak I have created is.

I'm very grateful to the people who have supported me in its creation and have dived in to explore. Thank you to my parents, siblings, and friends for your excitement, encouragment, and your persistent question of when is the sequel coming out? (I'm working on it. I promise).

Thank you to those who gave me feedback on the manuscript--to Brendan, Alisha, and Nicole for beta reading *The Damned Ones*. This book wouldn't be as good without you. Thank you to my sister Emily and Dale for proofreading it. You both have sharp eyes.

Thank you to Agata Broncel for designing the cover. It's gorgeous as always.

A special thank you to you, reader, for taking a chance on an indie author like me. I wouldn't be able to do this without you.

And finally, thank you to God for blessing me with the ability to write and publish this book.

ABOUT THE AUTHOR

Mary K Gowdy is a fantasy author and poet. She's currently working on her epic fantasy series *The One and the Other,* the first book of which came out in 2020. She grew up in the South, received her bachelor's degree in Linguistics from the University of North Texas, and currently works with refugees. When not writing, she enjoys rock climbing, listening to metal music, and convincing people that poetry is nothing to be afraid of.

You can follow her on Instagram @marykgowdy or join her email list at https://dl.bookfunnel. com/4um0k5w6nj and get *The One-Sided Coin* as a free download

www.ingramcontent.com/pod-product-compliance
Lightning Source LLC
Chambersburg PA
CBHW032225050726

47591CB00001B/272